# Matt Gargan's Boy

# Matt Gargan's Boy

**BY ALFRED SLOTE**

**J. B. LIPPINCOTT COMPANY**
**PHILADELPHIA AND NEW YORK**

U.S. Library of Congress Cataloging in Publication Data

Slote, Alfred.
  Matt Gargan's boy.

  SUMMARY: A major leaguer's son feels threatened when a girl
tries out for his baseball team and his divorced mother becomes
interested in the girl's father.
  [1. Baseball—Fiction. 2 Divorce—Fiction] I. Title.
PZ7.S635Mat   [Fic]   74-26669
ISBN-0-397-31617-8

FOR BARBARA SEULING

# 1.

MY NAME IS Danny Gargan. You haven't heard of
me, of course. I'm only eleven years old. But you've
probably heard of my dad. He's Matt Gargan,
catcher for the Chicago White Sox, and the best
catcher in the American League.

A lot of people ask me what it's like to have a big
league catcher for your father, and I tell them it's
great. You go to ball games for free, you sit behind
the dugout, and you can get pretty near as many au-
tographed balls as you want. And not just White Sox
balls either. I've got an Oakland A ball, a Brewer
ball, a Yankee ball, and a Baltimore Oriole ball. Dad
says this year he'll have more time and he'll get me
a ball from every team in the major leagues.

The reason he'll have more time I guess you

know if you're a fan. Dad's kind of at the end of his career. He doesn't play regular anymore. He's down in the bull pen most of the time. He told me privately that he figures this may be his last year. In a way I hope it is and in a way I hope it isn't.

I hope it isn't 'cause I'd like Dad to play forever. I like going to the games. I like watching him on TV.

But in a way I hope it *is* his last season 'cause I have the feeling when it's over he'll move back to Arborville where Mom and I live.

You see, my folks are divorced. My mom hasn't remarried. Neither has my dad. Mom didn't want to be a "baseball widow," as she put it, and I guess there were other things too. Anyway, they've been divorced for three years. I'm hoping that when Dad's career is over he and Mom will quietly get back together again. That's why I figure one of my main jobs is to keep Mom away from single men who'd want to marry her. This sounds funny, I know, but it can be done.

Like, there was this gym coach from the high school who'd known Dad for years. He was a bachelor and he kept coming around.

He's an OK guy. His name is Rusty Hills. He took Mom golfing or to basketball games, and I always figured a way to go along with them.

"Hey, Rusty, can I come along?"

Rusty would get all embarrassed. He didn't know how to turn me down. He'd stammer and finally say, "Sure, I guess, Danny."

Mom would smile. She never minded me coming between her and Rusty. It took me a long time to find out why. Finally, one day I asked her why and she said, "Danny, Rusty Hills is a nice man. But I don't love him. And I never will."

Which made me feel bad and good. Bad because I got the idea that if Mom ever met a man she did love, she wouldn't let me come along on their dates. Good because Rusty could be useful in keeping Mom free for Dad.

Rusty coaches the junior varsity baseball and basketball teams at the high school. In summer he's the assistant manager at the university golf course. He told me that when I was sixteen I could get a summer job there cutting grass.

I told him I thought he was a great guy.

Rusty beamed. "I wish your mom felt that way, Danny."

"She does. I think Mom really likes you."

You should have seen Rusty's eyes light up when I said that. "Do you really think so, Danny?"

"I know so, Rusty."

So he kept coming around. Mom would say, "I wonder why Rusty Hills keeps asking me out. I've told him a dozen times there's no future for us. He just won't quit."

I grinned. Not with me encouraging him, he wouldn't quit. As long as I had Mom paired with Rusty, she couldn't find anyone else and she'd be free for Dad.

That was my game plan. It was a good one. The only trouble was, it didn't work.

# 2.

IN THE OPENING GAME of the baseball season, our team, Delson's Market, was playing the Dairy Queens. They were the worst team in the league. Maybe because they tried too hard. Rumor had it that the Dairy Queen store gave them free Dairy Queens after each victory. Last year they were 2 and 14. I guess they were a pretty cheap team to sponsor.

Last year I'd one-hit them and Lou Salmon, our left-hander, had two-hit them. They were the same team as last year and figured to be no problem.

We were playing over at Rawson Junior High field. Rawson Junior High is on the west side of town. It's a pretty poor field, with a really bumpy infield that gives our guys fits. The other bad thing about it is Mrs. Smith. She's a cranky lady whose house isn't too far from the first base line. Any foul ball that drops into her yard she keeps. There's no arguing with her. And no time to jump the fence and get it. She's out faster than most kids can move, snatches up the ball, and disappears inside her house. No one knows what she does with those balls. Someone said she was going to open up a foul ball store someday. She could. All I know is that our coach, Mr. Harmon, once told me to ease up on my fast pitches because the other team was swinging late and we were down to two balls. It was a bad field to play on, any way you looked at it.

The only good part about it was that it was close to where Mom worked. Mom's the summer school librarian at Rawson. But when I told her the opening game was at Rawson, she said, "Good, then I can get to some of it."

"What do you mean, 'some of it'? It's right outside your window."

"I know that, Danny, but the new coordinator of school libraries wants to go over my library that day."

"Well, when you're done, bring her along too."

"She's a he."

"A he librarian?"

"Yes."

"Well, bring him along."

Which is what she did.

It was the bottom of the third, and I was sailing along with a no-hitter. We were two runs up on the

11

Dairy Queens, and Gayl Tinsley, their pitcher, was at bat. Behind me, my team was chattering away.

"Humpty Dumpties, Danny, that's what they are," sang out Leo Reilly, our second baseman. He and Warren McDonald, our left fielder, made the most chatter. Maybe it's because they're the smallest guys on the team.

At shortstop, Pete Gonzalez, our captain, put out a soft steady line of, "Fire it, Dan. Fire it, Dan. Fire it, Dan. . . ."

At third, Ed Farkas pounded his glove and yelled, "No stick, big Dan. No stick, big Dan."

At first, George Steinbrunner was usually pretty quiet. Once in a while he'd clear his throat and say, "Yup, lookin' good." That's practically a speech from George.

From the outfield, the chatter was less clear. Warren McDonald in left yelled things like, "Let the bum hit it, Danny." Warren loves catching fly balls. He can't hit beans, but he's death on flies.

In center field, Joe Tuttle says things I never understand. Like, "OK, man, what not get him, huh?" At least that's what it sounded like to me on the pitcher's mound.

In right field, Tucker Harmon, the coach's son, shouted tough talk, even though he's not very tough. He shouted things like, "In one ear and out the other." Or, "Stick it in his eye, Dan." If I did, Tuck would be the first one to run to the batter to help him.

Our bench is a lively one. A lot of our subs, like Simple Ulmer, whose name is really Simon but everyone calls him Simple for obvious reasons, and Charley Campbell, would be starters on other teams.

The chatter I like best though comes from my catcher, Sid Grayson. Sid is big and comfortable and makes a nice easy target for me. His voice is deep and soft, and he just calls out for me to pitch to his glove. "Pitch to my glove, man," he calls out. That's all Sid ever says, but it's enough.

Dad came in from Detroit one afternoon and watched us play and he was impressed with Sid. "The boy's got the size and the instincts," Dad said. Sid is also smart. He never gets rattled. He has a memory like an elephant. He can always remember what we'd got the guy out on the last game. He can remember pitches I threw a year ago.

Right now, Sid hunkered down and made his target low for Tinsley. Gayl was an OK hitter but they were batting him eighth just so he wouldn't have to feel responsible for bringing in runs and could concentrate on pitching. He liked high pitches. Low pitches he usually pounded into the ground.

"Pitch to my glove, man," Sid called out softly.

I rocked, kicked, and fired right to the glove for a strike. Tinsley was waiting for his pitch. Well, he'd wait a long time.

"Way to chuck, Dan," Mr. Harmon called out. Our bench whistled and clapped.

The infield talked it up and so did the outfield. Sid settled himself down and wiggled one finger for the fastball and again made his target low. Again I fired low and this time Gayl swung. He golfed it but only got a piece of it and arced it high and foul past first base.

One for Mrs. Smith, I thought. First of the season. But it didn't drop into her yard. It rolled past the fence.

"Out of play," the plate ump called. Out of play on the right field side was an imaginary line straight out from Mrs. Smith's fence.

Tucker Harmon chased the ball. I watched him and it was then that I saw Mom. She was walking across the grass from the school. She wasn't alone. She was with a man I'd never seen before. He had gray hair but he wasn't old. He was tall. They were talking and laughing.

"Ball in, Danny," Mr. Harmon called out.

I looked away from Mom and the stranger just in time. Tucker had really pegged it in. I stuck my glove up to protect myself and caught it. I might have been beaned if Mr. Harmon hadn't called out.

"You OK, Danny?" Pete Gonzalez asked from shortstop.

"Sure," I said. I spat and wiped my forehead and watched Mom and this guy come closer and closer. I rubbed the ball up. They were walking along the first base foul line. Mom must be telling him that I was her son because he looked over at me, interested.

"Batter up," the ump called out.

Tinsley stepped in.

"What's the count, ump?" Ed Farkas asked from third.

**14**

"0 and 2."

"One more, Danny."

"Way ahead, Dan."

I looked in at Sid. He wiggled one finger and placed his target low and outside. He wanted me to waste one. I nodded. Mom and the man stopped walking. They didn't want to be moving while I pitched. They didn't want to distract me.

Heck, when I'm pitching nothing distracts me.

I went to a full windup and threw the ball low and wide. Tinsley was protecting the plate. He reached across it and tapped the ball foul, a little skidding grounder that shot off the end of his bat. Their first base coach went over to field it, but the ball never reached him. This guy with Mom, this stranger, leaned over and barehanded it and with an easy motion flipped it across the diamond to me.

"Sign him up," Simple Ulmer yelled from our bench.

I stared at the man. He winked at me and then he and Mom walked the rest of the way around the backstop and climbed up into the stands between third base and home.

All the guys know my mom. She comes to all the games. They were probably wondering who the guy was. I was wondering too.

My eyes followed them. I watched them sit down. He didn't act like a librarian. Librarians couldn't field ground balls.

"C'mon, Gargan," the ump called out to me. "We got a batter in the box."

"Wake up, Dan," Mr. Harmon called out.

"Way ahead, Dan," Pete said.

"No stick, Dan," Warren McDonald called in from left field.

Mom said something and the man with her smiled. My next pitch hit Tinsley in the elbow.

"Take your base," the ump said.

"He didn't try to get out of the way, ump," Ed Farkas yelled.

Tinsley, glad to get on, lucky to get on, trotted down to first base rubbing his elbow. Sid came out to the mound. He looked a little worried. I never hit batters.

"How's it going, Dan man?"

"I'm OK," I said, annoyed. "The ball got away from me. That's all." I held my hand out for the ball.

"Rick Cummins is at bat," Sid said. "He can't hit. Just get it over. Don't worry about Tinsley. He won't steal."

"I'm OK," I said.

"Sure," Sid said.

I pitched pretty well from a stretch. I didn't have the quick move to first that our lefty, Lou Salmon, had, but it was good enough to keep most guys close. And Tinsley wouldn't be going. Not with them two runs behind.

Having a guy on first woke up the two or three fans that the Dairy Queens had in the stands. Losing teams don't bring out fans. Most of the people watching the game were for us. Mom and the man were sitting there watching me. Mom smiled at me. I ignored her. I spat and stepped on the rubber.

Sid set his target over the heart of the plate. Cummins was a little guy who swung with a choked bat. He'd never got a hit as long as I could remember.

I went to my stretch. Tinsley took a little lead. Not too much. He wasn't very fast. I looked at him and then fired to the plate. Just off the strike zone.

"C'mon, Dan," McDonald called in from left field. "Let him hit it."

The man with Mom was talking to her. She was nodding. Was he criticizing the way I pitched from the stretch? Not too many people stole on me. I didn't pick off many runners, but not too many stole on me.

My next pitch was in the dirt. I'd held onto it too long. My stride was too short. I wasn't coming around in a rhythm. I'd taken my eyes off Sid's glove.

"C'mon, Danny. This guy is a nothing hitter," Leo said from second.

"Fire it, Dan," Pete said softly. "Fire it, Dan."

Mom smiled at the stranger.

My third pitch was six feet over Cummins's head. Sid jumped and barely got his glove on it. Tinsley took second and made a turn as if to go to third. Sid fired down to Farkas and Tinsley held at second.

Mr. Harmon stood up as though he were going to come out to the mound. Ed Farkas called time and walked the ball over to me.

"What gives, Danny?"

"I don't know."

Pete, Leo, and Sid came to the mound.

Leo said, "If you walk a punk like Cummins I'll never speak to you again, Gargan."

"Cummins has never even hit a foul ball," Ed said.

"He got a foul tick two years ago," Leo said.

I grinned. I appreciated what they were doing. They thought I'd tightened up and were trying to relax me.

"I'm OK," I assured them.

Ed put the ball in my hand. "Just throw it to Sid, for Pete's sake."

"For my sake too," Leo said, and they laughed. I laughed too.

"You want to try to pick Tinsley off second?" Sid asked.

"He won't take enough of a lead," Ed said.

"We'll pick him off anyway. Right, Danny?" Leo asked.

The way we work our pickoff play is, after the pitcher brings his hands to his chest, he and the infielder covering second start counting, "One potato, two potato, three potato, four." On "four," the pitcher turns and throws while the infielder jumps for the bag. Even though we practice it a lot, it never works. Just the same, now was the time to use it, when my pitch to home wasn't working.

"Batter up," the ump yelled, breaking up our meeting.

The guys went back to their positions. Sid called for the fast one down the middle. I looked back at Tinsley. Not much of a lead. I looked at Sid's glove. Then I went to my stretch and brought my hands to my chest. One potato, two potato . . . Mom stood

**18**

up and the man with her stood up. Were they leaving? No, they were moving up a row. . . .

I heard Leo break for the bag. I was way behind. I'd stopped counting. Throw hard, I thought. I whirled and threw as hard as I could to make up for my break in the rhythm. I threw as wild as anyone could throw wild to a base. The ball was in the dirt, way off to the second base side of the bag. I'd wrong-footed Leo, who was cutting toward the bag. The ball went skipping into center field. Tinsley took off for third and made his turn. Joe Tuttle came in fast. He charged the ball, scooped it up, and, still running, fired the ball to me as the cutoff man. I whirled with it, but Tinsley was scooting back into third.

Mr. Harmon yelled, "What's going on out there?"

Now the Dairy Queens were up and yelling. They got even more excited when my fourth pitch to Cummins was in the dirt.

Mr. Harmon called time.

# 3.

"MEN ON FIRST and third, no outs," Mr. Harmon said. "Danny, you're beating yourself."

"I know."

"Does your arm hurt? I don't want to keep you in there if it's hurting."

He was thinking this was the first game of the season and maybe my arm wasn't ready. It was a little cool yet and cold weather could be tough on a pitching arm.

But it wasn't my arm. Sid knew that. I was throwing as hard as I'd ever thrown.

"My arm's OK, Coach."

Mr. Harmon looked into my eyes as if he suspected I wasn't telling him something. I'd pitched in four practice games already and had given up a total of only four or five hits.

20

"What is it then, Dan?"

"I don't know."

"Sid, how does he look to you?"

Sid hunched his bearlike shoulders. "He was going good, Mr. Harmon, and then all of a sudden—whammo!"

"I don't think Danny's coming around the way he usually does," Leo stuck his two cents in. "He's not kicking high either."

Mr. Harmon frowned. He'd asked for Sid's advice and now he was also getting Leo's. Too many cooks. "Dan," he said, "relax and just chuck away. Let them hit it. You've got the best fielding team in the league behind you. Your rhythm will come back. Don't force the ball. Just play catch with Sid. OK?"

"OK."

"Nobody out. Men on first and third. Where's the play?"

"Home on a ground ball if we got the play," Leo said. "Otherwise, we play for two."

"Right. Everyone in. I don't want that run on third to score. Danny, if you can, keep your pitches low so they'll hit them into the ground. But don't walk anyone!"

He patted my arm and left the mound. Sid was the last to leave. He looked worried. "Just keep your eye on my glove, Dan," he said, as though I hadn't been doing just that.

Their leadoff batter was up. A kid named Sinelli. I knew him from Saturday morning basketball in the fall. He was a good basketball player but not really a baseball player. The only thing he had going for him was his legs. He was fast. He got on base on drag bunts, or squibbly grounders that you had to handle with care. But if you threw chest-high fastballs at Sinelli, he couldn't bunt or beat the ball down onto the bumpy infield.

Sid gave me the high target. He remembered too! Behind me, the guys were in tight to cut off the run at the plate. Tinsley took a couple of dancing steps off third. I didn't think he'd go. He wasn't the type. Kids who try to steal home are a special breed. They become motorcycle daredevils when they grow up. Tinsley was going to be a lawyer or something like that.

But Cummins might be trying to steal second to give Tinsley a shot at home. Well, let him. I wasn't worried about Cummins. I wanted to keep Tinsley on third.

I looked at Tinsley and then over at Cummins and then back at Tinsley. He was ten feet off the bag. But so was Ed Farkas. Tinsley, as a matter of fact, was standing in a direct line between me and Mom and that man. The man was leaning forward, watching me as though he'd never seen a pitcher in trouble before. Mom was watching me too.

I fired to Sid. Way too high. No one was moving. Cummins faked a run for second and then ducked back as Sid faked a throw at first. Tinsley went back to the bag at third. Sinelli stepped out and rubbed some dirt on his hands. He did that because he saw major leaguers do it on TV. Rubbing dirt never helped a nonhitter hit the ball. But the way I was going, nonhitters didn't even have to swing to get on base. The Dairy Queens' bench was shouting at me; their fans, all two of them, were clapping their hands rhythmically. Mr. Harmon was frowning. But Lou Salmon, our other pitcher, was still sitting down. I knew Mr. Harmon's plan had been for me to go the first four innings and Lou the last three.

Sid fired the ball back to me. Their first base coach was talking to Cummins, probably telling him to go on the next pitch and get the tying run in scoring position. Cummins kept nodding. I looked at Sid. He'd seen the conference too. He nodded.

Sinelli stepped in. Sid wiggled one finger and held his glove up for the chest-high fastball. Tinsley came down the line shouting, "Here I come. Here I come." And then he stopped.

I fired. Sinelli ducked. The ball was over Sid's head, crashing against the backstop. I stood there paralyzed.

"Cover home, Dan," Mr. Harmon shouted.

But by the time I woke up, it was too late. Tinsley had scored. Cummins was on second and Sinelli had two balls and no strikes on him.

Lou Salmon got off the bench and began to warm up. I stood there feeling dumb. My father was a major leaguer, but you'd never know it to watch me. Losing your control was one thing. Things like that happened. But not covering home on a wild pitch was unforgivable.

Pete came over from shortstop. "Stall," he said.

I nodded. My job now was to give Lou time to warm up.

Sid walked the ball out to the mound. "Hey, everyone, tying run's on second. Take your time, Danny." He'd given up on me too.

The stranger with Mom stood up. He said something to her and she to him and then he worked his way down out of the stands. He jumped the last step down. Our eyes met. He winked at me and then he walked off, out of the field, through the gate onto the street.

Suddenly, a load was lifted off my shoulders. Mom sat there alone, as always, watching me. Sid was squatting, as always. The guys were chattering automatically, as always, and Sinelli, who was no hitter, was standing in there.

Sid called for the fastball at the belly button. He was taking no more chances. I checked Cummins on second and then wheeled and gave it to Sid's mitt, belly button high. Sinelli never moved his bat off his shoulder.

"Strike," the ump said.

Our guys yelled.

Before Sinelli knew what hit him, I threw two more blistering fastballs and he was out of there.

That quieted down the Dairy Queen bench. Lou Salmon sat down. Mr. Harmon relaxed.

I got their number two batter to pop up to Steinbrunner at first and struck out their number three batter. We hustled in.

"Boy, Danny," Leo said, "you sure had me worried there. What happened to you anyway?"

"I don't know."

Mr. Harmon made room for me on the bench. "Feeling better?"

"Yeah."

"Things like that will happen, first game of the season." He checked his lineup card. "McDonald, Harmon, Reilly," he called out. "Boys, let's get some runs. Let's give Danny a cushion."

They gave me a cushion all right. Before that half inning was over, we'd scored five runs. As it turned out, we didn't need any of them. I shut the Dairy Queens out with only one hit and Lou mopped up the last three innings, and they didn't get a hit off him. The final score was 9–1, and we even threw our gloves up in the air when Ed Farkas squeezed a pop foul for the third and final out.

Mr. Harmon was one of the few coaches that made his players go over to the other team's bench and shake hands at the end of the game. This wasn't hard to do when you won, but pretty difficult when you lost. It may have been one of the reasons we played so hard. It's no fun being a loser, and less fun being a good loser.

After we shook hands, Mr. Harmon sat us down on our bench.

"All right, we beat an easy team today, and we got away with a lot of mistakes. Even for the first game of the season, there were too many mistakes. Ed, you were swinging at bad pitches all afternoon. So were you, Tucker. Leo, outfielders call off infielders on pop flies. Don't go crashing into Tuttle again. Pete, I don't want you missing any more 'take' signs. Danny, you got away with that wild streak in the third inning, but don't let it happen again. Concentrate. All of you. You didn't look sharp at all."

25

"Pinch me," Leo whispered. "Who won that game anyway?"

"We won, Leo," Mr. Harmon, who had good hearing, snapped, "but only because we were playing a last-place team. Friday we're playing Harts Trucks. We beat them 1–0 last year and 3–2. One-run games. If Danny has that wild streak again, if Leo crashes into Joe, if Ed swings at bad pitches, if Pete ignores signs, we'll lose 10–0. All right, practice tomorrow at Sampson Park at four thirty. Who cannot make it?"

No hands went up.

"Good. I'll see you then."

"Hey, Mr. Harmon, can we go for Dairy Queens now?"

Mr. Harmon smiled. "You're starting early, aren't you, Warren? It's a long season. You'll have to beat a better team than the Dairy Queens for me to take you for a treat. If we beat Harts on Friday, then the treat's on me. I'll see you tomorrow. Tucker, get the bag."

Tucker Harmon hefted the equipment bag and followed his dad to their car.

"How do you like that?" Leo said. "We win 9–1 and get bawled out."

"We deserve it," said Pete. "Those guys should never have got one man on base against us. Look at them."

We looked across the diamond. The Dairy Queens hadn't even had a team meeting, but there they were goofing around in the Rawson parking lot, laughing and ducking behind cars. You'd have thought they'd won and we'd lost. Teams like that are born losers.

"Who needs a ride?" Warren asked. "My dad's here."

"So's mine."

"Mine too."

"Danny?"

"My mom's here."

"Hey, I saw her," Leo said. "Who was that guy she was with?"

"You got me."

"Did you see him scoop up that foul grounder? He looked pretty good to me."

"He was lucky," I said.

The guys laughed.

I knotted my baseball shoes together, looped them around my neck, picked up my glove, and went over to where Mom was talking with Mrs. Tuttle and Mrs. Grayson.

"Hello, dear."

"Nice game, Dan," Mrs. Grayson said. "You pitched very well."

I shrugged. "Not too good. Sid was good though. And so was Joe."

Mrs. Tuttle and Mrs. Grayson both smiled. "Joe says the team depends on you, Dan," Mrs Tuttle said.

"He's nuts. Can we go home, Mom?"

"Mrs. Grayson and Mrs. Tuttle are taking their cars to the Dairy Queen. Do you want to go too?"

"No, thanks."

"Sid gets very thirsty, catching," Mrs. Grayson said.

The women all laughed. Though what was funny about that I don't know. You do get thirsty catching. It can be a very dry and dusty position.

"I'll see you next game, Marge."

"Friday. Good-bye, Nancy."

"The baseball season is upon us all," Mom said cheerfully. "Good-bye to regular dinner hours."

"Isn't that the truth?" Mrs. Tuttle said.

I walked alone to our car, which was a VW bug, and got in. Mom would come along later. She just didn't know how to say good-bye and leave. Women don't know how to leave each other. A guy says "see ya" and leaves. A girl says "good-bye" and stays.

Finally, Mom arrived and got in the driver's side. I told myself to be cool about it, but I wasn't. I hadn't the patience to wait until we were home. I started right off. Even before we were out of the parking lot.

"Well, who was he?"

"Who?"

"That man you were with."

"Oh, you mean Herb Warren. He's the new library coordinator."

I didn't believe her. "He doesn't look like a library coordinator."

She laughed and backed the car out and we went out the school drive. "Danny, dear, just what does a library coordinator look like?"

Not like him, I thought, but didn't say anything.

Mom waited till traffic cleared and then we

turned right on Huron Avenue. I tried another approach.

"He's pretty old, isn't he?"

"All of forty-seven."

That was old. Dad was only thirty-eight. Old for a major leaguer, but not too old to come back to Arborville and help coach our team.

"I bet his kids are older than me."

I was fishing for information and Mom knew it.

"As a matter of fact, he has two daughters. One older than you. I believe he said she was sixteen. And one just your age."

I relaxed. He was married. Nothing to worry about after all.

"Well," I admitted, "he did scoop that ball up pretty good."

Mom laughed. "I asked him about that. He said he used to play a lot of baseball. Nothing like your father, of course, but he played in high school. Besides being a librarian, he writes books."

"What kind of books?"

"Story books. Like the kind in your school library."

"Have I read any?"

"I don't think he's ever got any published."

"He couldn't be much good then."

"I told him I'd read one of his stories and give him a librarian's opinion. I think it's marvelous knowing a writer."

As long as he was a married writer, I agreed with her.

"He loves baseball. He tells me his daughter

Susie is a very good baseball player. She's the one your age."

"I hope you told him we don't let girls play in our league."

Mom smiled. "Well, Susan Warren may be on a team very soon."

"What team?"

"Herb doesn't know yet. He's meeting with Mr. Davis, the league president, tonight about it."

"Well, she won't get on our team because Mr. Harmon won't let a girl on it and neither will any of the other coaches. Those men aren't coaching to coach girls. And besides, none of the guys will play with her. I wouldn't pitch to any girl."

"You probably won't have to."

"What do you mean?"

Mom had one of her amused little smiles on her lips. "Why, dear, if she gets on your team you wouldn't be pitching to her."

"Cut it out. She won't get on our team and that's that."

"She might help your team. Herb says she's good, Danny. In Dayton last year she was the best fielder on the team. Herb says—"

Herb says. Herb says. She never knew this guy till a little while ago and suddenly it was Herb this and Herb that. I stayed cool though. Even a guy named Herb could come in handy. He was married. He had kids. He was old. He had gray hair. Heck, he was even safer than dumb old Rusty Hills. I ought to be happy old Herb was around.

I decided I would be.

So as we drove home, I changed my tack and I allowed as how I didn't mind at all if girls got on boys' baseball teams, as long as they were on other guys' teams. Mom said I was narrow-minded, and I said that was OK too, only I liked calling it "being in a groove." Mom said that if I didn't watch out, the groove would become a grave. I told her to please drive carefully. She laughed and I laughed and it was like it always was driving home after a ball game, feeling good because you've won and won big.

# 4.

YOU ALWAYS WANT to make a good feeling last. All ball players are like that. You want to forget the defeats as fast as possible and slowly relive the victories.

When we got home I grabbed a can of pop out of the refrigerator. Mom smiled. "All right, but just one. Remember, we're having dinner."

"Sure."

There's nothing like cool pop after a ball game. Dad always had a couple of cans of beer after a victory. When they lost, he didn't want anything. He wouldn't even want to talk. Just be by himself. But after they'd won, Dad would pop a beer and stretch his legs and go over the game with us.

I popped my pop, turned on the TV, and

stretched my legs out. If I got the right kind of show on TV, I could sort of not-watch it and let my mind run. It's hard just to sit and relive a game. It's easier when you can not-watch TV.

What I got on the tube annoyed me though. It was a comedy about one of those big fat happy families growing up on a farm in Illinois with lots of brothers and sisters getting into scrapes that got a lot of laughter out of the canned-laughter sound track, but didn't get any laughter from me. So I switched channels and caught an old movie with about six hundred girls kicking their legs in the air, and a big band and stars twinkling down. That was so far out, it had so much nothing to do with me, I could not-watch that better than anything else. And I could relive our ball game.

It was fun letting the cold pop dribble down into my body and remembering how I struck out Sinelli who was first up in the first inning. I got him on three straight pitches. Their number two hitter was a string bean named Hoskins. I got him leaning to the outside, thinking outside corner, and then I slipped a quickie inside on the knees. The ump called him out and Hoskins turned around to bellyache but Sid said, "C'mon, man, you were fooled and you knows it." And that stopped Hoskins 'cause he knew deep down he'd been fooled. Sid could always talk to batters deep down. That's part of what made him a good catcher. He knew what guys were thinking.

Good old Sid. Wouldn't it be terrific if he and I could go up to the majors together. Dad had gone up with a high school pitcher, only the pitcher hadn't made it. But now I was the pitcher and Sid was the catcher. Funny that I hadn't become a catcher like Dad. But when he came back to Arborville to live, it would be even better because he could catch me. And if he could hold up in the majors another six or seven years, we might be the first father-and-son battery in major league history. But that was really daydreaming.

"Danny!"

"Yeah."

"Are you washed up?" Mom asked.

"Washed up? Man, are you kidding? I haven't finished my pop yet."

"I'm not 'man,' " Mom said. "I'm your mother, and dinner is ready, so go wash up."

I hadn't even got through the first inning and we had to eat already.

"Now!" Mom added.

Which she didn't have to since I move for coaches and mothers.

"Can I bring my pop to the table?"

"Yes, but you have to drink milk too."

"No sweat."

"Move. Now!"

"I'm moving. I'm moving."

I washed up. I used a washcloth. I like to get dirty, but I also like to get clean. When I got to the table, Mom was sitting there waiting for me. It was a big table. We'd had it in Chicago. I told Mom she ought to trade it in for a new one, a smaller one. The

34

two of us didn't need a big table, but she said she liked the table and wasn't going to sell it.

So we sat on opposite ends and kind of slid things along to each other. Breakfast and lunch we ate in the kitchen. But Mom insisted on dinner in the dining room.

"Turn your hands over," she commanded.

I did.

"Good. Do you want to say grace or do you want me to say it?"

Ordinarily Mom says it. But when Dad was with us, he used to say it. For some reason I heard myself saying, "I'll say it," even though I couldn't remember anything to say right off.

Mom put her head down. I put my head down too and stared at the glass of apple juice sitting in the center of my plate.

"Go ahead, Dan," Mom said.

I grinned. "Rub-a-dub-dub, thanks for the grub. Yea, God!"

I looked up. Mom still had her head down. "Now say it properly," she said quietly.

I put my head down. "Thank you, O Lord, for the food we're about to eat, for our good health, and . . . for the good victory today over the Dairy Queens. Amen."

"Amen," Mom said, and she looked up with a smile. "I hadn't known God was rooting for your team."

"He wasn't rooting for them, that's for sure. What's for supper?"

"Fish."

"Fish?"

"Yes, fish. We haven't had fish in a while. It's cheap and it's good. Finish your juice and I'll bring it in."

"Fish hasn't got as much protein as red meat. Dad says ball players should eat red meat."

"Rich ball players."

"Did you know how to cook before you got married?"

"No. I had on-the-spot training." Mom took my juice glass and hers into the kitchen.

"Did Dad ever get sore at you?"

"Usually it was the other way around. I'd get sore at him."

"Because you were a lousy cook?"

"That's right."

"It doesn't make any sense. Why did *you* get sore?"

Mom laughed. She put the fish onto a big platter. Even though it was just the two of us eating, she acted like we were a big family and needed serving plates and stuff like that.

"I got mad because it didn't matter to him whether I cooked well or not. He couldn't tell the difference between good food and bad. He couldn't tell the difference between a good book and a bad one. He couldn't tell the difference between good music and bad, between good people and bad. All he cared about and knew about was baseball."

"That's all I care and know about."

"You're eleven."

"I won't change."

"God help you then. Or perhaps I ought to say, God help your wife."

"I'm never getting married. Hey, that's enough fish. It's too much. Why did you make so much?"

"It's hard to buy fish for only two, Danny. Everything is packaged for four or five people. I almost asked Herb to get his girls and bring them over for dinner. We have enough here for four or five."

"Don't you think his wife would mind?"

"He's a widower."

"What?"

I almost dropped my fork. Suddenly I could hear every sound in the room: the whirring of the electric clock, the hot-water heater noises coming up through the air duct, the buzzing of the fluorescent light in the kitchen.

"Herb's a widower. His wife died three years ago."

Herb this and Herb that. It was a different ball game now. I felt a little sick.

"Do you want some lemon?"

"No."

I'd have to go at this slowly. Not show her I was disturbed.

"What did she die of?"

"Cancer, I think."

"That's too bad."

"Herb's been bringing up the girls by himself. He's doing a marvelous job."

"How do you know?"

"They do well at school. The older girl is a

painter. The younger one is the good athlete. Herb spends a lot of time with them. They go camping together every summer. He does most of the cooking, though Sallie, the older girl, is getting to be a good cook, he says."

"They sound like they're a pretty happy family."

"Yes, they do. How's your fish?"

"It's OK."

"Why don't you eat it then?"

"I'm not too hungry."

"You were a moment ago."

"I'm not now."

"Put some lemon on it."

"I'm OK. How long are they going to live in Arborville?"

"I don't know. They just got here a week or so ago."

"I mean, is he here for a year or is it a permanent job?"

"It's a permanent job."

"Oh."

"How about some more broccoli, Danny?"

"I'm fine."

"You're not eating anything."

"I'm never hungry after a game."

"Except for hamburgers."

"This . . . uh, Mr. Warren, is he your new boss?"

"I guess you could call him that."

"Then you shouldn't get too friendly with him. People'll think it's 'cause you want a raise or something."

Mom thought that was funny. She laughed. "I

wouldn't worry about that, Dan. The number of people who are concerned with the lives and careers of school librarians is very, very small."

Try another approach, I told myself.

"Don't you think it's a funny thing for a man to be? A librarian? I never heard of a man librarian before."

"They exist. Herb's one."

"I'd think a real man would go into coaching, like Dad will when he quits playing."

"I see," Mom said. "Real men coach but other men don't?"

"I don't mean that, but librarian work is women's work, and coaching is a man's job."

"Danny, there are women who coach and men who are librarians, and, furthermore, what makes you so sure your father can coach when he's done playing?"

"You're kidding. He's a major league baseball player. He knows everything about the game."

"That doesn't mean he can teach it."

"It's sure a good start. Besides, Dad's a catcher. That's the smartest position on the field. Dad'll get dozens of coaching offers. In the majors too. I just hope he comes back here."

Mom was silent. She looked at me quizzically. "Do you think about that a lot, Dan?"

"All the time."

"I'm sorry."

"What're you sorry about?"

"I think you're letting yourself in for a big jolt. Your father won't come back to Arborville."

"How do you know?"

"I know. He's used to bigger things now."

"That doesn't matter. He's from here. Whenever I go to visit him we always talk about Arborville. I bet he does come back and I bet he coaches a Little League team. I bet it's our team."

Mom sighed. "How about eating your fish?"

"I can't eat anymore. I'm not hungry. Can I be excused?"

"What about dessert?"

"I'm really not hungry."

"Do you feel all right?"

"I feel fine." I got up from the table.

"Where are you going?"

"To my room."

"And do what?"

"Lie down."

"Please shower first."

"Sure."

"And Danny . . ."

"Yeah."

"Don't start fiddling with the radio. You can wait till they come into Detroit and hear them play on a Detroit station."

"If I play the radio, I'll play it quietly."

I left her sitting there. Her and her widower Herb Warren. Boy, didn't that come out of nowhere? Herb this and Herb that and suddenly she wanted to invite him and his daughters over for dinner. Daughters? It was like being caught in a rundown. Well, they hadn't tagged me out, and if I played it right, they never would.

I took a shower and put on shorts, new T-shirt, and sneakers. I threw my uniform onto the floor of my closet. If I left it in the bathroom or out in the open in my room, Mom would snatch it up and wash it and I wouldn't see it again for days. Besides, I liked having my uniform a little dirty. It would never get as dirty as Sid's. Catchers play in the dirt. Dad's uniforms always had a lot of dirt on them after a game.

I lay down on my bed and turned on my radio. Mom hated it when I tried to get the White Sox games from Chicago. I couldn't really get Chicago too clearly, so I had to turn the volume way up and a lot of static came through. I could always hear the game through the static, but all Mom heard was the static, and it got her mad. It also got her mad that I practically knew the White Sox schedule by heart. They were playing the Royals tonight in Chicago. Tomorrow, the Brewers were coming in and the game was scheduled for national TV.

The Chicago station that broadcast the Sox games was around 90 on the dial. I turned the sound way up. Sometimes you could get it good, sometimes you couldn't. It depended on the atmosphere. Once, I got them playing the Yankees in New York and I could hardly hear anything, and then all of a sudden I heard Harry Caray, the Sox announcer, say clear as a bell, "And it's a home run for Matt Gargan, and look at that big old veteran run around those bases. Everyone's on their feet clapping for the big popular catcher. . . ."

That got me so excited. It was like God tuning in

my radio, wanting me to stay in touch with my dad. No matter what Mom said, I knew that Dad would come back someday. All we had to do was be ready for him. Show him he was welcome, that this was his home.

"Danny!" Mom yelled. She opened my door. "Will you turn that down?"

"Sorry."

"You have a phone call."

"I didn't hear the phone ring."

"How on earth could you have?"

I turned the radio off. A bad night for a long-distance ball game. I answered the phone in Mom's room. It was Leo Reilly.

"Gargan," he said, "you won't believe what's happened to us . . ."

I knew right away what had happened. I knew it right down to my toes. I knew sure as sure that Mr. Herb Warren's daughter was joining our team. And that meant he'd be coming to all our games from now on—and probably with Mom.

"A girl," Leo said disgustedly. "The first girl in the league, and she has to come on our team. Mr. Harmon says it's 'cause they want her to be on a team that other teams won't razz. But we'll get razzed all right. Everyone's pretty sore. We're all over at Pete's house. The back porch. Can you come over?"

"What're you guys doing? Having a team meeting?"

"Kinda."

"Why didn't you call me?"

"We're calling you now."

"Why so late?"

"We'll explain it when you get here. Can you come?"

"I'll be right over."

I hung up.

"Mom, I'm going over to Pete Gonzalez' house."

Mom was sitting in the living room with a cup of coffee and the evening paper. She had the hi-fi on playing softly.

"All right, Dan," she said. "Don't be back late."

"I won't."

"Was that Leo?"

"Yeah. Listen, don't do the dishes. I'll do them when I get back."

She smiled. "There aren't that many, unfortunately."

"Ha! You may be the only woman in America who wants a lot of dishes to wash."

"I do," she said.

The phone rang again. I had an idea who it might be. It was. Before I went out the front door, I heard Mom say, "Why, Herb, that's wonderful. Of course she should be excited. They're a fine bunch of boys. And I know Danny will look after her. I'm sure he'll—"

I took off for Pete's house. I ran hard.

# 5.

PETE LIVES in a big old white house on Forest off Wells. It's one of those houses that kept getting added onto as the family got bigger. The family kept getting bigger. Mrs. Gonzalez kept having babies and Mr. Gonzalez kept adding rooms. He could do it too. He was a builder. And a really nice guy. Quiet. Not a ball player but a nice man. Pete's like him—quiet, and sure of himself. Which is why he's captain of the team. Whenever the team's got troubles, the meeting's always over at Pete's house.

I biked across the park toward Forest Avenue. It was dark in Sampson Park now. No ball players except for one crazy tennis player who was pounding balls against the backboard. I don't know how he could see the ball. I could barely see him. But that's how tennis players are.

There were other noises in the park. They came from the shelter. There's a shelter that's really a warming house in winter when there's ice skating. On spring and summer nights the seventh and eighth graders hang around the shelter—boys and girls. I don't know what they do, but I do know none of the guys are ball players.

As I biked across the middle of the park, bumping over the rutty clay infield of the smaller diamond, I heard the pounding of the tennis ball on my left and kids laughing and squealing under the dark overhang of the shelter to my right.

"Hey, who's that?" a girl's voice asked, and I knew she was referring to me.

"That's Gargan," a boy said. "Hey, Gargan, how's the big leaguer's kid?"

I looked over at the shelter. I wasn't afraid of anyone. A bunch of giggles went up. I decided to ignore them.

A lot of people know me that I don't know. Mostly because of Dad. When I come to bat in a game, I can sometimes hear people in the stands say things like:

"That's Matt Gargan's boy."

"Built like his old man, ain't he?"

"Gonna be a good one too, I hear."

A lot of kids hearing stuff like that might choke, but I loved it. I loved being Matt Gargan's boy; it gave me a goal, something to shoot at. I was going to be a major leaguer too someday. It could be done.

Dad had done it. I had his blood inside me. I'd make it too.

I biked past the "cool" kids and over Diamond No. 2, past the swings and the slides off the right field foul line. There were some kids fooling around on the slides. A girl called out, "Hi, Danny."

It was a girl from my class. I ignored her.

"Stuck up," she said, and then she and another girl giggled. That's what girls do. They go to the park at night and fool around on kid stuff like swings and slides, and giggle.

I biked out of the park and onto Wells. At the corner of Forest and Wells I heard our guys before I saw them. They were making a lot of noise on what's usually a quiet street. I bet they were real popular with the neighbors and with Mrs. Gonzalez who has lots of little kids to put to bed early.

The guys' bicycles were parked all over the Gonzalez' front lawn, but the main action was in the backyard. I left my bike next to Warren McDonald's and walked around to the back. The guys were playing whiffle ball. Some of the little Gonzalez kids were in the game too. Tucker Harmon was chasing Pete's younger sister Rose with a balloon filled with water. She was screaming happily. From one of the Gonzalez' second-floor windows another sister was playing the radio loudly and leaning out the window watching and grinning. It was a terrible-looking team meeting and I told Leo so.

"We were waiting on you, man," Leo said. "Pete, Danny's here."

**46**

"OK, guys," Pete said, "game's over. Tucker, throw that balloon away. Rose, Joey, the rest of you kids beat it. We got to finish our meeting."

"How come you started without me?" I asked.

Pete looked embarrassed. "Well, we weren't sure where you'd stand on this, and I wanted to know where the rest of the guys stood. They're kind of blaming you."

"For what?"

"For the girl," Ed Farkas said. "She wanted to be on our team. Not on anyone else's team—ours. It's because of you, Gargan."

Every face was turned toward me. They thought I actually had planned this thing.

"She knows you," Leo said.

"I've never seen that girl in my life!"

"Well, her dad knows your mom. That's why we're stuck with her."

"No one's blaming you, Danny," Pete said.

"Sure you are."

"No, we're not, but we got to find out where you stand on this girl."

"I'd like to stand on her all right."

The guys laughed.

Pete didn't. He turned to Tucker. "Tell Danny what this guy told your dad and what your dad told him."

Tucker was embarrassed. It's tough being the coach's son. You get to play more than you deserve sometimes, but you pay for it by being a go-between.

"Well, this man Mr. Warren told Dad he knew your mom and that you were the only eleven-year-old kid they knew in town."

"It's not true. They don't know me. I never saw that man till today."

"Well, that's what he said. My dad told him we don't need anyone. We got a set team. First-place team. We got guys like Simple here and Charley who don't start for us and who'd be the main men on another team. Mr. Davis, the league president, came over with Mr. Warren. He said he knew that, and that was why he thought we ought to take this girl on our team. 'Cause girls were starting to play in boys' baseball leagues all over the country and it was only a matter of time before it happened in our leagues and Arborville was going to have to fall in line and the easiest way to make everyone fall in line would be if Delson's Market, the best team in the league, let a girl on it. Then all the others would too."

"What a lot of bull," Leo said.

"He also said she's a really good player."

"More bull," Ed Farkas said.

"And lastly that she's a friend of Danny Gargan's."

"And that's the most bull of all," I said.

"Well," Tucker said, embarrassed, "Dad didn't know what to do, so he said well, she could come to practice tomorrow."

"Is she gonna play against Harts on Friday?" Leo asked.

"If she can play. Dad's supposed to get her a uniform if she makes the team."

"Does she have to make it or is she on it?" Pete asked.

"I don't know. Dad's not sure either. Mr. Davis wants him to put her on it. I don't know."

"She's on it," Pete said flatly. He turned to me. "It's up to you to get rid of her, Danny. You're the reason we got stuck with her. 'Cause your mom knows her dad. So it's up to you to go over to this guy's house tonight . . . Mr. Warren, and tell him we don't need Mary Jane on our team."

"Her name's Susie," Tucker said, like a dope.

"What's the difference?" Pete said. "We don't need a girl on our team. You got to tell him that, Danny."

" 'Cause my mom knows her dad, I got to do it?"

"Well, he'll take it coming from you. He's probably counting on you to look after her."

"Bowwow, Gargan."

"Hoo-wee, Danny."

"Meetcha at third base, honey child."

"Shut up," Pete said.

The guys shut up.

"She's coming on our team because of you, Dan," Pete said. "So she'll leave because of you."

"Pete's right, Danny," Ed Farkas said. "You got to tell her old man she'll never even get a chance to play. We've got guys like Simple and Charley who hardly play. How's she gonna play?"

"That's the thing," Pete said. "You tell him it's

not fair to her. Got that, Danny? It's not fair to her."

"Right," Leo said. "We got to think of her."

"Absolutely right."

They all beamed at each other. What a bunch of phonies. I didn't want that girl on the team any more than they did. In fact, probably a lot less for a reason I wasn't going to tell them, but I wasn't going to be a phony about it. I couldn't be.

"Listen, you guys know what to say. You say it."

"It wouldn't work coming from us, Danny," Pete said, "but coming from a guy whose dad is a major league ball player . . . coming from a guy whose mom works for this girl's dad, who's supposed to look after her, he'll understand that."

"Suppose he doesn't understand. Suppose he says he doesn't care. Suppose he says he wants her to play for us whether I look after her or not."

Silence. They looked at each other, bewildered. They hadn't gone that far in their thinking.

"Well," Ed Farkas said kind of grimly, "there's more than one way to get rid of her."

"What do you mean?"

"If she plays second, I might just barrel into her, breaking up a double play."

Warren McDonald laughed. Sid looked a little disgusted with Ed, but the rest of us thought about it seriously.

"Or maybe," Ed went on, "I'll put a skull tag on her if she comes sliding into third in a practice. We can make life pretty awful for her and force her to quit. 'Course, she might get hurt. If she does, that'll be on your conscience, Danny, 'cause you wouldn't try to get rid of her first. She might get really hurt."

I grinned. Now I was responsible for the girl's safety. A girl I'd never met in my life.

"What do you say, Dan?"

"I say Farkas is funny. Heck, I don't see anything wrong with being tough on the girl. If she's gonna play in our league, we ought to be as tough on her as other teams will. I'm all for Ed putting skull tags on her."

That kind of took the wind out of their sails.

"Aw, Danny, quit fooling around," Leo said. "You're the only one who can do it, and you know it. What do you say, yes or no?"

They were all looking at me. What they didn't know was that I had the best reason of all to do it.

"OK, I'll do it. Where's he live, Tucker?"

A cheer went up.

"Way to go, Dan."

"That's our man."

"Over on East Baker Place."

"You think he's home now?"

"Only one way to find out, man."

"He's home," Tucker said. "My dad was just on the phone with him. Let's go."

"Are you guys coming with me?"

"Sure," Pete said. "That'll show him we're behind you. But you do the talking."

"And remember," Leo said, "we're being fair to her. If she comes on our team she'll never get a chance to play."

"And if she's good," Farkas said, "there are teams that need her more than we do."

"We got it both ways."

"Made in the shade."

"And if that don't work," Leo said, "you got to make it clear to him that the guys just don't want a girl on the team."

"And not just the guys, Danny," Ed said. "You. *You* don't want her."

"Ed's right," Pete said. "You got to make it clear to the man you won't be able to look after her. You're our big pitcher. You got enough to worry about just pitching."

"Hey, that's enough gabbing," Warren McDonald said. "Let's shove off."

They got up and ran to the bicycles in the front yard. I followed them slowly. I was thinking: Our team wouldn't fall apart if a girl came on it. If anything, Mr. Harmon would only play her in the last inning. He'd probably stick her in right field for an inning, and I'd throw inside pitches so no one would hit it out to her. That was no problem. Nor would any razzing we got from other benches be a problem.

The problem would be in the stands. It would be my mom sitting with her dad. It would be the two of them coming to the games together and then sticking together after the games. They'd already disturbed my concentration in today's game. It would only get worse.

I'd be a spokesman for the guys, but I'd also be a spokesman for myself. I wasn't doing it just for them. I was doing it for me. And I was doing it for Dad.

"Danny, are you coming or not?" Leo yelled from the street.

"You're darn tootin' I'm coming," I yelled back. I got on my bike and took off after the guys. By the time we hit Packard, I was ahead of them all.

# 6.

EAST BAKER PLACE isn't a Place at all. It's a wide one-way street running from Granger Avenue into Stadium Boulevard. It's a shortcut for people wanting to get to the high school. It's also on a direct route to the A&P, the bowling alleys, and a lot of other stores on the other side of Stadium Boulevard. I guess by now you get the idea it's a crummy street to live on.

The houses aren't too bad, but they're mostly rented out. People move to Arborville. They rent a house on East Baker Place while they look around to buy a house in a better part of town.

If you live on East Baker Place you go to Sampson Park School, where we go, but you don't really live in the Sampson Park neighborhood. I mention this because I saw this as another possible argument against the girl coming on our team. We're neighborhood teams, by and large, and this isn't really our neighborhood. The trouble is, Joe Tuttle lives on White Street, not far from here, and also there's no team in this neighborhood. There used to be one in the nine-year-old league, but it broke up. But Mr. Warren didn't know that and we didn't have to tell him.

We biked down Granger in the dark. There must have been fourteen of us, and I wonder what the people sitting on their porches thought. Fourteen bicycles going by in the dark and kids yelling back and forth. When we turned onto East Baker Place though, everyone shut up except Pete.

"Which is their house, Tuck?" he asked.

"It's Kelly Craigin's old house. The brick one next to the one on the corner."

"Hey, what happened to old Craigin?"

"He moved to Ohio."

"Maybe this girl'll move there."

"No way. She just came from there. Ain't that right, Danny?"

"How do I know?"

I was going to resist every attempt to link me with this girl whom I'd never seen and knew I didn't like.

"That's Craigin's house," Pete said.

"And there's the girl," Ed said.

"Gee, she's big," Leo said. "She's bigger than Steinbrunner."

A really tall girl was standing outside the house

near the curb. She was waiting for someone. Us? We braked our bikes.

"Maybe she'll play first," Warren said, giggling. "Then you infielders can throw as high as you like."

"She's gonna have to be able to hit good," George Steinbrunner growled. "I never seen a girl could hit good."

"But man, what a reach. Did you know she was that big?"

"No," I said, and grinned to myself in the darkness. That had to be the older sister. Mom said Mr. Warren had a sixteen-year-old daughter too and that had to be her. But I wasn't going to tell them I knew that. If I did they'd just figure I really knew this family. I didn't know them. I didn't want to know them.

The older sister was looking our way, but right through us. She wasn't interested in us. And then a car honked behind us and pulled around us and over to the curb in front of her. A high school kid was driving. She got in and they drove off.

"Hey, she's leaving."

"She's got a boyfriend who drives."

"Maybe she ought to be our coach," Warren said. And that got some nervous laughter out of the guys, but no one really knew what to say.

"What do we do now, Danny?" Pete asked.

Then I had to tell them the truth. "That wasn't her, Pete, I don't think. She's supposed to have a sixteen-year-old sister. I bet that was her."

Whistles, laughter. "Well," Leo said, relieved, "that's better anyway. I'd hate for the biggest guy on our team to be a girl. Should we lock our bikes?"

"In this neighborhood, yes."

"Nobody'll steal fourteen bikes."

"A guy with a truck could."

"Aw, shut up, McDonald."

"Quiet," Pete commanded. "We're not going in. Just Danny is going in."

"That's right. It's Danny's deal."

"Give 'em heck, Dan."

"Remember, man, we're right behind you."

"About a mile and a half behind."

"Just tell him the truth, Danny," Pete said quietly. "Remember, we don't need her."

Pete came up the steps with me. I rang the bell. The curtains were drawn so you couldn't see in. The door was solid too. No glass frames you could peek through.

The outside light went on. My heart skipped a beat or two. I hadn't expected to be scared. But suddenly I was. The door opened, but instead of tall, gray-haired Mr. Warren, there was this girl standing there, a little shorter than me, ponytail, pug nose, freckles, and chewing gum. She looked at me and then at Pete and then past us at the guys on the sidewalk on their bicycles. Her face had absolutely no expression on it.

I cleared my throat. "Is this Mr. Warren's house?"

She nodded.

"Can I speak to your dad?"

"What about?" she asked. She was suspicious. She wasn't making any moves to let us in.

"About baseball. I'm Danny Gargan. This is Pete Gonzalez."

"Oh," she said.

"Who is it, Susie?" a man's voice called from somewhere inside the house.

"Danny Gargan and the kids from his team."

Pete frowned. He was captain and leader. He would have liked the team to be called "Pete's team." No one ever did call it that. I grinned a little, watching Pete.

"Ask them in. I'll be right there."

"You want to come in?" the girl asked.

"Naw. I'll stay out here."

"He'll go in," Pete ordered.

I shrugged. "I guess I'll come in. They'll wait outside."

"OK," she said, and she shut the door behind me. I stood there. "Come on in," she said. "We're still fixing things up."

I followed her into the living room. It was pretty small and it was a mess. Pictures were stacked up on chairs and leaning against the sofa. There were unopened cartons all around. Even after it was fixed up, it wouldn't be much of a living room. They'd want to move out of a house like this pretty quick, to a house like ours, if they could find one.

She saw me looking at the pictures. "They're my sister's. She's a painter."

"Yeah?"

"She just left."

"Yeah."

"She's got a boyfriend."

"Yeah."

"Is that really your team outside?"

"Yeah."

"Is that all you say is 'yeah'?"

"Yeah."

"What time is practice tomorrow?"

I looked at her. "Why do you want to know?"

She frowned. "I got to know what time it is if I'm gonna be there."

She was cool, I thought.

Best thing now was to stall. "I don't know."

"You don't know what time practice is?"

"That's right. I don't know."

"I don't believe you."

"So don't believe me."

"Back home we had practice every day on off-game days. We practiced at five thirty."

"Yeah?" I wasn't interested and I hoped my tone told her so.

"Yep," she said. "Are there lots of girls in the leagues?"

"None in our league, though I hear there's one girl in the ten-year-old league."

"What position does she play?"

"The bench."

She blushed. I grinned. "I hear she sits on the bench real good," I said.

Her mouth got grim. "I played second base and, sometimes, shortstop in Dayton."

"You must've had a killer team."

"We finished in third place."

"Out of how many teams?"

"Ten."

"That's just over fifty percent ball. We haven't lost a game in two years. We've won the championship the last two years."

"That's what Dad says. He says—"

"Aha, someone mentions my name and here I am," Mr. Warren said. He came in from what I guess was the dining room. He was in the middle of painting because his pants had white paint on them. So did his hands, and there were smudges of paint on his face. He probably had paint in his hair too, but you couldn't tell because he had gray hair. My dad would have hired a painter and had it done right.

"Hello, Dan," he said, and held out a hand with wet paint on it. "We haven't met formally. I'm Herb Warren."

"Daddy," the girl said, "look at your hand!"

"Oh . . . you're right. What am I doing? Here, Dan, I'll give you an elbow to shake. That's how the French shake hands when their hands are tied up. They extend their elbows."

"I don't believe that," she said. "He's always making things up."

Mr. Warren pretended to look hurt, but he was grinning. "Susie, I couldn't possibly make something like that up. And I don't *always* make up things anyway. There are times I tell the truth. How did your game come out, Dan?"

"We won 9–1."

"Good. I figured you'd settle down. The first game of the season can be a rough one. You've got a nice motion out there on the mound."

"My dad's a major leaguer."

"You see, Susie."

Susie blushed. "He told me your father was a major league ball player, but I didn't believe him."

"She never believes me," Herb Warren said, pretending he was sad. "It comes, I guess, from my making up too many stories."

"Dad's a writer."

"I'm a librarian."

"No," Susie Warren said, "he's an author, but he can't make any money being an author so he's a librarian."

"And I don't make much money doing that either, but we're happy."

"I'm not," Susie said. "I wanted to stay in Ohio. Our Little League team there would have won the pennant this year. We could have gone all the way to the state finals."

"Your Little League team will win here."

"This isn't even official Little League here, Daddy. It's Recreation League baseball."

"It's as good as Little League," I said, annoyed. Here she hadn't even seen one of our games, not to mention played in one, and she was knocking our brand of baseball. Typical girl-thinking.

"Baseball's baseball," I said. "You either play it good or bad."

"Absolutely right," Mr. Warren agreed. "I never heard it put better in my life. The uniform doesn't make a ball player; the name you give your league doesn't guarantee whether it'll be good or bad ball."

"We'll see," Susie said.

"Yes, you will," her dad said.

And I knew that right then and there was when I should jump in and tell her she wouldn't see. She wouldn't see 'cause we didn't want her on our team.

She wouldn't see 'cause there was no chance a girl was going to break into our lineup. I should have said that right then and there, but I just couldn't. The two of them were pretty close, and he was kind of on my side in the argument, so how could I break in? I couldn't.

I was saved by the bell. The doorbell.

"I wonder who that can be," Herb Warren said.

He opened the front door. There was Pete, and behind him Leo and Farkas and Tucker Harmon and Sid and George and Warren and all the guys.

"Have you boys been out there all this time?" Herb Warren asked.

"Yes," Pete said. "We figured Danny would get it said by this time."

"Get what said?" Herb Warren asked.

I looked down at the floor. I felt Susie Warren's eyes on me.

"Danny's supposed to tell her we don't want her on our team."

"Oh." Herb Warren turned to me. "You didn't say anything about that, Dan."

I swallowed. "I . . . uh . . ."

Susie ran out of the room. She ran up the stairs. We heard a door shut upstairs.

"Well, boys," Herb Warren said softly, "let's sit down and talk about it. You don't mind sitting on the floor, do you?"

"No," Pete said grimly.

"I'll wash my hands and I'll be right back. Come on in, all of you."

They all came into the house.

# 7.

"NICE GOING, DANNY," Leo said after Mr. Warren had left the room to wash up.

"What the devil were you doing here all this time?" Pete asked.

"Listening to them. It was hard to get a word in."

"I bet."

"You got any idea how long we were out there?"

"I know."

"Were you chicken to tell her?"

"Cut it out, Leo."

"What difference does it make?" Ed Farkas said. "We're here now."

"That *was* her, wasn't it, Danny?"

"Yeah."

"I think she's kind of cute."

"Hey, listen to Tucker."

"Well, she's prettier than Reilly anyway."

"What's her position?"

"Second."

"Leo, you've had it."

"Any time a girl beats me out for second I'll hang up my spikes," Leo said, glaring around him.

"Simmer down, all of you," Pete said. "No girl's coming on our team. And Danny should have told her that."

"I couldn't."

"You sure you don't want her to play with us?"

"Sure I'm sure."

"Look, it's kind of tough on Danny," Warren said. "With his mom working for that guy."

"That's got nothing to do with it," I said. "If anything . . ." And then I let it drop because Herb Warren had washed his hands and was coming back into the room.

He smiled at us. "All right, boys," he said, "I won't remember all your names, but I'd like to hear them anyway. Danny, would you do the introductions?"

I wondered why he was doing this. Maybe he wanted to slow down the action, take charge of things, show us who was running the show. From upstairs, I could hear nothing. I wondered what Susie Warren was doing. Probably crying on her bed. Girls did things like that.

I made the introductions one by one and when I was done, Mr. Warren said, "Fair is fair. I'm Herb Warren. We just moved here from Dayton, Ohio. I

**64**

have a daughter named Sallie who's sixteen and a daughter named Susie who's eleven. Now, before we go any further, would you boys like something to drink? Some ginger ale?"

No one expected that. Everyone was mistrustful. Was he trying to suck up to us?

"No, thanks," Pete said.

"Do you mind if I wet my whistle a little? Painting makes a body thirsty."

"No. Sure. It's OK, I mean."

He went off again and came back with a bottle of ginger ale. He was really in charge of us now. We all felt it, and there wasn't anything fourteen of us kids could do against one smart adult. And he was smart all right. You had to give him credit for that.

"All right," he said, after taking a drink from the bottle, "I take it there's a problem about Susie making your team."

"She *can't* make it," Ed Farkas growled. "That's the problem."

"I'll take it, Ed," Pete said smoothly. He turned to Mr. Warren. "We heard from Tucker Harmon here that your daughter's been put on our team. We came over to ask her to quit because we got no room for her, Mr. Warren. We got guys on our team like Simple Ulmer and Charley Campbell who could start for any other team in the league and barely play for us."

"I heard that," Herb Warren said pleasantly. "I heard Delson's Market is a terrific team. One of the best ever in Arborville. I also was told there were no girls playing in the eleven-year-old league. Well,

Susie's a ball player. And she wants an opportunity to play ball. Maybe she won't when she's sixteen. I don't know. She doesn't know either. But she's a ball player right now. She was a good one back in Ohio and she'll be a good one here in Michigan. So far, no one's told me the game's played any differently here. You still have to run, hit, and field. Susie can do all those things. Now the question comes up: Whom does she play for? A bunch of last-place junkers who already think they're terrible and will fall through the bottom of the league if a girl comes on? How could they take the bench jockeying? They're too awful to let a girl play with them.

"Or does she do it the hard way and the right way? Try to get on a team that plays heads-up ball? A proud team? A team that knows it's good, so that if a girl makes the club they're sure enough of themselves to take it in stride? If Susie can make a championship club, then she'll have done something for herself and for other girls who might want to play baseball in this town."

Mr. Warren paused. He looked around at our faces. He was wondering if we understood what he was saying.

"That was my thinking when I went to the league president, Mr. Davis, and asked him what was the best team in the league."

"You mean," Leo asked slowly, "it wasn't 'cause you knew Danny's mom?"

"Not at all. I met Danny's mom for the first time a few days ago. It was a coincidence that her son was the pitcher for this team. A coincidence that you had

66

a game right outside her school library. But, I'll admit, I think it's a lucky coincidence because Susie doesn't know anyone her age in Arborville and I think it's always nice to have friends in a strange town."

I was off the hook anyway.

"So there you have it, boys. The rest is up to you."

"What do you mean?" Pete asked.

"I mean, you can either welcome Susie or not. If you're dead set against her, it's crazy for her to try to play for you. But I figured you boys were good enough ball players, sure enough of your talents, to let a girl try out for your team. Boys who weren't that good would be afraid to."

I think everyone finally understood what he meant by a good team being willing to take on a girl, but not a poor team. But they were still suspicious.

"I get that part," Ed Farkas said. "What I don't get is, is she trying out or is she on our team?"

"Trying out," Mr. Warren said firmly. "You've got a practice for tomorrow, Mr. Harmon told me. Susie would like to come to it and show you what she can do. If you don't think she's good enough to make your club, she'll quit. She'll look for another team. I promise you that. Now, does that seem fair?"

"Suppose she thinks she's good enough but we don't?"

"I don't think that will happen. Besides, your coach is there and he'll settle it."

"Will you be there?"

"If I can get away I'd love to be there. I always get a great deal of pleasure watching Susie play ball."

"You'll be wasting your time, Mr. Warren," Leo said boldly. "There's no way a girl is gonna make our team."

Mr. Warren smiled. "Will you dare give her a tryout?"

"Has she got shoes?" Pete asked.

"Of course."

"OK. I'm willing. What do you guys think?"

No one said anything. Most of the guys were embarrassed. Pete looked at me. "Danny?"

There was no way I wanted to give her a tryout, but I couldn't very well come out and say so. Besides, I couldn't see her making our team anyway. She'd get a real tryout, a tough tryout, the kind of tryout Ed Farkas threatened to give her a while back. And if no one else gave it to her, I would.

"It's OK with me."

"Practice is at four thirty at Sampson Park," Pete said.

"Good," Mr. Warren said, smiling. "That's all we ask." He got up and went to the bottom of the stairs. "Sue, could you come down a second?"

"What for?"

"I want to tell you about tomorrow."

She came right down. She'd probably been sitting at the top of the steps listening. She hadn't been crying on her bed at all. She was some kind of snoop. She didn't look fussed or anything. She was chewing bubble gum, her hands were in the pockets of her jeans. She had an I-don't-give-a-hoot look on her face.

"Susie, there's no point in introducing you to all these boys because you'll be meeting them all tomorrow. There's been a misunderstanding. They thought the league president Mr. Davis had *put* you on their team. I made it clear to them you wanted to *make* the team. So tomorrow's practice will also be a tryout for you. OK?"

"OK," she said, and her face had no expression at all. She didn't even look at us. She just looked at her dad and went on chewing gum. She was a character, I thought.

A flicker of a smile crossed Mr. Warren's face. "Tomorrow at four thirty it is. Sue, do you know where Sampson Park is?"

"No."

Some snickers went up.

"That's our home park," Pete explained. "We're a neighborhood team from around *there*."

He hit "there," and I think Herb Warren and his daughter Susie got the point.

"It's right up Granger," Tucker Harmon said, embarrassed. "You just go up Granger, cross Packard, and keep going till you come to Lincoln or Baldwin. Turn left on either street and you run into the park."

"Thank you, son. I think we'll be able to find it."

There was a moment of awkward silence. No one knew how to break it off.

Finally Pete stood up. "Well, uh . . . nice meeting you. See ya," he said to Susie.

"See ya," everyone said, and followed Pete out

the door. I was the last to leave, not because I wanted to be, but because I was the farthest from the door. Mr. Warren put his hand on my arm, detaining me. He looked into my eyes.

"We don't expect any favors, Dan."

Holy cow, I thought, he thinks I'm on his daughter's side. He thinks I'll groove pitches for her tomorrow. If he only knew!

I shook my head. "No favors," I said.

"Good. See you tomorrow. Good night."

"Good night." I didn't say anything to her. She didn't say anything to me. When I left, she was still standing there on the bottom step of the stairs, chewing gum, her hands in her pockets.

The guys were on their bikes down at the corner of East Baker Place and Granger. They were waiting for me.

"What'd he say to you, Dan?" Leo asked.

"He said he didn't want any favors for her tomorrow."

"You're darn tootin' no favors," Ed said.

"He's OK though," Tucker said. "I think he's an OK guy."

"He's not trying to get on our team," Leo reminded him.

"He looks like an old ball player," Sid said.

"An old high school ball player," I said with contempt.

"That's pretty good right there," Warren said. "Mr. Harmon never even made his high school team."

"He didn't try out," Tucker said angrily. "Dad ran

track in the spring. He could have made the baseball team of his school if he'd wanted to."

"I didn't say he couldn't. I just said he didn't play
high school ball."

"It's the way you said it, McDonald. You said—"

"Come on," Pete said. "Quiet down." And, to me,
he added, "That girl'll be nothing but trouble. She's
causing trouble already and she hasn't even tried
out."

"Pretty smart of him to say we were good enough
to let her play with us," Sid said, grinning.

"Yeah," Steinbrunner muttered. "I didn't get
that."

"Well, everyone else did," Leo said.

"Well, I didn't," Steinbrunner growled.

"That's 'cause you're dumb."

"Who're you calling dumb, Reilly?"

"You see," Pete said. "The girl will cause trouble.
She's not getting any favors tomorrow . . . from
anyone. Right?"

"Right," everyone said, even Tucker.

"Danny?" Pete asked.

"What?"

"Let's hear you say 'no favors.' "

"I said it."

"I didn't hear you," Pete said. "Say it again."

What dumb-dumbs, I thought. They really
thought I might want her on the team so Mom and
Mr. Warren could come to our games together. How
little those guys understood anything.

"No favors," I said softly. "No favors at all from
me."

And the way I said that left no doubts in their minds. We biked home slowly. It was a nice night. Tomorrow would be fun too.

Mom was sitting in the living room reading. She took off her glasses when I came in.

"Where've you been, Dan?"

"With the guys."

"I called the Gonzalez' house a half hour ago. They said you'd all gone somewhere."

"Well, we did." I hesitated. What harm would it do to tell the truth? "We went over to Mr. Warren's house."

"Herb Warren?"

"Yeah. The guys don't want his daughter on our team."

Mom put her book down. "I hope you didn't hurt that girl's feelings, Danny."

"Gee, Mom, we just want to protect her. We've got a good ball club and if she gets put on it, there's no way she'll ever play. Mom, we got guys sitting on the bench who—"

"I know. But that's no reason she can't try out for your team."

"Well, that's OK. I mean, we didn't know she was going to try out. We thought she'd been put on the team. Tomorrow she gets her tryout. And she'll get a real tryout." I tried not to grin, thinking of some of the things that could happen to someone in a tryout.

"Was Herb . . . Mr. Warren there?"

"Sure. He was painting. He talked to us."

"What did he say?"

"Aw, Mom, how can I remember? A lot of things."

"What do you think of him, Dan?"

Warning signals flew up inside me.

"I don't know. Can I get some pop?"

"Don't you think he's nice?"

"There are nice guys all over. Nice guys finish last."

"Baloney."

"No baloney. It's the truth. And if you like nice guys, Rusty Hills is nice."

Mom put her glasses back on and turned her book up. "I think I've finally discouraged him, at any rate."

"Huh?"

"And don't you encourage him anymore, please. Rusty told me you'd told him I loved his coming around."

"I thought you did."

"You thought nothing of the sort, Danny Gargan. Go ahead and have some of your pop. But once in a while I'd like to see you come in and ask for milk."

"Milk cuts your wind. Dad told me that."

"Nonsense. You need milk for growing bones."

"My bones are fine. When I go sliding into Susie Warren at second, she'll know how good my bones are."

"I hope you're not going to be mean to her."

"Just tough."

Mom removed her glasses again and looked at me. "That sounds mean, Dan. Can't you just once look at what this means from her point of view?

73

She's a girl, she's alone, she's lonely, she doesn't know anyone, she—"

Mom stopped. She wasn't talking about Susie Warren, and we both knew it.

"I better get my pop," I said.

Mom nodded. She put her glasses back on and started reading. She was embarrassed.

# 8.

I GOT TO Sampson Park at four. Three little kids were playing on our diamond, if you could call what they were doing playing. They stopped and watched me sit down on the bench.

"You want to play with us, Gargan?" asked the pitcher, a red-headed kid I'd never seen before in my life.

"Naw, I don't play with little kids."

"Your Dad gonna make the all-star team, Danny?" the catcher asked.

"I don't know." I'd never seen him before either.

"Do you got his autograph?" the kid playing shortstop, third, and left field asked.

"What do I need his autograph for? He's my dad. You kids better quit gabbing and start playing

75

'cause in a little while we're taking over the diamond."

"You got it reserved?" the pitcher asked. He was
maybe nine years old and probably knew more
about reserving diamonds than about playing on
them. It was sad.

"Sure we got it reserved."

"Is she on your team?" the catcher asked. He
pointed off to his left, past the elm trees between
the parking lot and the tennis courts. Susie Warren
was sitting against a tree, her knees drawn up, her
glove on her knees. She was wearing a baseball cap.

"No, she ain't on our team."

"She says she is."

"Well, she's not. And you kids better play 'cause
our guys are coming."

That got them moving. The red-headed kid
started throwing balls to the catcher, and the catcher
would catch the ball once in a while and throw it
out on a fly or on the ground to the shortstop–third
baseman–left fielder, who would catch it once in a
while and throw it back to the pitcher. They could
have used a bat, some other players, and a coach.

"Can I sit down?"

I'd seen her coming over out of the corner of my
eye, but I pretended I hadn't.

"It's a free country," I said.

Susie Warren sat down and then pounded her
glove.

"Let's see it."

She handed it to me. It was a pretty good glove,

well broken in, used a lot. I wondered if it was her dad's, but she'd probably be insulted if I asked that. I pounded the pocket and handed it back to her. She had on baseball shoes. I don't think I'd ever seen a girl in baseball shoes before. Her sneakers were on the grass in front of her. Tennis sneakers. Her uniform was a T-shirt and jeans. Her cap was blue with the letter *B* on it.

"What was the name of your team in Ohio?"

"Becker's Express."

"Trucks?"

"Yes."

"That's who we're playing tomorrow. Harts Trucks. They're the number two team. We're number one."

She blew a bubble and snapped it. Her expression didn't change. She acted like she didn't care, if she even heard what I said.

"Does your sister play ball?"

"No. She used to ride horses."

"Lots of girls around here do that. That's a girls' sport."

She acted like she didn't hear me.

"What other sports do you play?"

"Just baseball."

"How about basketball?"

"Just baseball," she said, and blew another bubble. It got bigger and bigger. I have to admit she was pretty good at it. Joe Tuttle was the best bubble blower on our team, but this girl would push him.

"I guess you're a real specialist."

She looked at me to see if I was kidding her. I didn't let her know. She could put on a pretty good poker face. So could I.

"I do OK," she said flatly.

"In Ohio maybe."

"You got a ball?"

"No. Tucker brings the equipment bag. The ball bag's in there."

"We had our own balls too."

"Where's yours then?"

"Still packed away. Dad hasn't unpacked our athletic stuff yet."

"Ours?"

"Yeah. His and mine. He still plays. Softball mostly."

"That's a rotten game."

She snapped her bubble. "You ever play it?"

"In recess we play it all the time."

"That's recess softball," she said contemptuously. "That ain't softball."

I grinned. Hot dog, I thought.

"What's funny?" she asked.

"You are."

"No, I'm not."

"Yes, you are. Softball's bunk anyway. I've seen the softball leagues down at Vets Park at night. It's for girls and men with potbellies."

She let the first part go, but stood up for her old man. "My dad doesn't have a potbelly."

"He will if he goes on playing softball."

"Bull."

"You'll see. What position you going out for?"

"Second base . . . maybe short."

"Forget shortstop. Pete Gonzalez plays there. He's captain. There isn't an easy position to make on our team. You'd be a lot better off trying out for a team that needs help. We don't."

"Yeah," she said, and snapped the bubble again. Nuts to her, I thought. Let her learn the hard way. There are people you can help and people you can't help, and this was one you couldn't.

"Is that our team?"

The Harmon station wagon had pulled into the parking lot and Tucker, McDonald, and Joe Tuttle were getting out.

Our team? That wasn't even worth answering. She'd never make Delson's Market. Not in a million years.

Mr. Harmon got out and wound down the back end, and Tucker and Joe pulled out the equipment bag. Then Tucker and Warren McDonald carried it together between them. I stood up. Across the park, near the school, I could see bicycles coming our way: Pete, Leo, George, Ed, Sid . . .

"Hey, Danny," Warren McDonald said, "who's your friend?"

"Funny man."

"Hello," Tucker said to Susie Warren. "How're you doing?" Tucker was kind of soft on her.

"OK," she said, without expression. She wasn't soft on him.

"Let's warm up," I said, and got out a baseball. "C'mon, Tuck, Warren, Joe. Let's throw."

I got them throwing right away with me, two on a

side. I ignored the girl. She stood up and watched us. Tucker kept looking at her, a little embarrassed. He asked me with his eyes and a little nod whether we shouldn't include her in and I shook my head.

While we warmed up on the sidelines, the little kids went on with their pretend baseball game. Mr. Harmon came over with his clipboard and the rest of the guys arrived on their bikes.

"You're Susie," Mr. Harmon greeted her.

"Yeah," she said.

"I'm Dale Harmon, coach of Delson's Market. Glad to meet you, Susie. Or is it Sue?"

"Either one's OK."

Some guy laughed, but no one said anything. I thought she blushed a little, but I couldn't be sure.

"OK, it'll be Susie," Mr. Harmon said loudly, warning us with the tone of his voice. "Susie, why don't you start warming up?"

Everyone had paired off and was throwing except her. The fact was, no one had offered to warm up with her. Mr. Harmon finally caught on. He took a ball out of the ball bag and tossed it to her and then looked around.

"Tucker," he said. "Warm up with the young lady."

"Yeah, go to it, Tuck," someone said.

Tucker turned red, but he left our game of catch and lined up with her. The way Mr. Harmon said "young lady" told me that although he wanted to be fair to her, he didn't know what to do about her either. No real man wants to coach a girl on a boys' team.

We all paused to watch Susie Warren throw a ball. She threw OK, like a boy, with her body and her hips, and she came down overhand and followed through. OK, no big surprise. That ought to be the least she could do. It would be another story when she started fielding and hitting and running.

We ignored her and went back to warming up. After about ten minutes Mr. Harmon called a stop. "All right, boys, let's get—" He hesitated. "Susie, I guess you'll just have to include yourself in when I say 'boys.' Is that OK?"

She nodded.

"Good. All right, let's get this tryout business over with right now. What's your position, Susie?"

"Second base."

"Bye-bye, Leo."

Mr. Harmon ignored the funny remarks. "All right, young lady, get out there at second and we'll see what you look like. Pete, get out to short. Ed on third. George, take first. Joe, go out and play center field in case any balls get through. Sid—"

"In case?" someone asked.

Mr. Harmon ignored it. "Sid, you catch for me. OK, let's get going. Kids," he said to the three little kids, "I'm afraid I'll have to ask you to leave now."

The three little kids had quit playing long ago. They were just standing there openmouthed, watching us. Now they ran off and sat down on the grass and watched us.

Mr. Harmon picked out a bat and looked over the infield. Out at second base Susie Warren kicked at the dirt, spat in her glove, and leaned forward.

"She looks like a ball player anyway," someone on the bench said.

"Anyone can spit in their glove," Leo said.

"All right, let's play for one, Susie," Mr. Harmon called out, and he tapped an easy ground ball down to second. My grandmother could have looked good on it. So it was no surprise when Susie Warren came in, scooped it up, and tossed sidearm to first. She had a nice motion out there. Steinbrunner fired it home to Sid and Sid, without pausing or thinking about it, fired it back to the bag at second base. She hadn't covered the bag. The ball went into center field. Joe Tuttle went down on one knee and fielded it and tossed it in to Pete.

"We always go back to the original base, Susie," Mr. Harmon called out. "We whip it around. It gives me a chance to see what your throw home looks like. So, when playing for one, we go second to first to catch to second and back to home. Got it?"

She nodded. If she was bothered by her lapse, she didn't show it. 'Course, maybe she didn't think of it as a lapse since no one told her, but it told you what kind of team she came from in Ohio if they didn't do that.

"Let's try it again. Playing for one."

He hit another easy ground ball down to second. She fielded it and flipped it to first. George to Sid. Susie was back at second, leaning forward, glove out. Sid fired it on one bounce to her. Her first hard play. She backed up a little and caught it cleanly—a nice play—and threw home. It came in on one bounce to Sid. Not a great throw. Not much steam on it. But it was accurate and would have got a runner. Leo didn't throw that much better.

"Ho, ho, ho, Reilly," Charley Campbell said.

Leo didn't say anything. His face was grim.

"It could be different in a game situation," I said to Leo. "With a guy sliding into her."

Leo nodded.

"Try it again," Mr. Harmon called out, and this time he hit it a little harder and into the hole between first and second. She moved easily, anticipating, grabbed the ball, and flipped to first. She was smooth for a girl.

Next Mr. Harmon started hitting balls to her right, and then to her left. He hit some pop flies and some line drives. They tried for two and he let her start the double play. Then he let Pete start it to see how she pivoted and fired to first. She was OK. On throws back to second when Pete was covering, she instinctively backed him up. She looked experienced out there.

"Relax," I said to Leo. "It's all nothing till you get men on base."

"I'm relaxed," Leo said to me, annoyed. "I ain't worried."

Mr. Harmon dropped a bunt down the first base line. It was too far for Sid to handle. George came charging in. He picked it up and fired to first. She was there. She'd been well coached in Ohio. She fired it back to Sid. George hustled back to get Sid's return throw and around the horn it went, George to her to Pete to Ed and back to George, and George fired it home to Sid, who flipped it up to Mr. Harmon. They looked good out there. It'd be hard for a stranger to know it was a girl out there on second.

After a few more ground balls, Mr. Harmon called a halt.

"Let's hit some. Susie, I'll let you bat second. Danny, you bat now and get your licks out of the way. I'll throw to you and then you'll throw to four hitters, then Lou will pitch and then Pete. Sid, get your equipment on. Tucker, get out in right field. Warren, take left. Susie, you stay at second till Danny's finished hitting. Then you're up. Leo, you go out to second when she comes in. Everyone gets five swings and you run the last pitch out. Let's look sharp now and concentrate. That's what we didn't do against the Dairy Queens. Baseball's in the head as well as out on the field. Concentrate on the ball. Bang the ball, field the ball, throw the ball. You ready, Sid?"

"Yup."

"Batter up, Dan."

I stepped in. I wasn't going to try to blast anything at second base. I wasn't that good a hitter to pick my spots like that, even though the coach was pitching. He threw nice easy fat balls, unlike Lou, who was always trying to sneak a cutie over on me. Which I didn't blame him for since I did the same to him when he came to bat.

I laced the first two pitches Mr. Harmon threw into left and left center. Then I tapped a grounder to Ed Farkas at third. My fourth pitch, I hit a long fly to center that I should have pulled into left—it would have been a home run. I had everyone backed up now. Susie was way back; so was George. Well, now was the time to see how she did, and I knew just what to do.

Mr. Harmon's fifth and last pitch to me floated up there. Instead of swinging away, I laid a bunt down the first base line. It was for George. Mr. Harmon wouldn't bother with it; it was too far for Sid. George came hustling in; I saw Susie cutting for first base. I sprinted like mad for first. Susie was stretching for the throw. It was going to beat me. It got there a half step before I did, but as I crossed the bag I gave Susie Warren a little hip, which sent her sprawling onto the grass. The ball squirted out of her glove. I made my turn and headed for second, for third, and circled the bases. No one made a play on me. She was sitting up as I crossed home.

Mr. Harmon was eyeing me. "What was that for?"

"She was blocking the bag."

"No, she wasn't."

"In a game situation that could have happened."

Mr. Harmon was silent. He turned. "You OK?" he asked her.

"Yeah," she said. "I wasn't expecting it."

"Danny's right though. That kind of thing happens in our league. Danny, go back to first. Let's try a little simulated game. Ulmer, you bat now. We've got no outs and a man on first."

"Don't I get five swings?" Ulmer asked. He hardly ever played and now he wasn't even getting his five swings. I had to laugh.

"You'll get them later," Mr. Harmon reassured him. "No one out. Man on first. Let's look alive."

**85**

Everyone grinned except Susie Warren. My bumping her had given Mr. Harmon the idea of how to work this tryout. I couldn't tell though whether Mr. Harmon was for me or against me. Whether he wanted to dissuade her from coming on our team or whether he really wanted to see how she performed under pressure. I guess maybe you could do both at the same time.

"All set, here we go."

I took a little lead off first. Mr. Harmon glanced at me and then went to his stretch position. I moved farther. I could read him good. Just to make sure he wouldn't catch me off, I leaned back toward first. But he wasn't testing me. He was testing her. He'd want me to go.

He threw home. I went.

"Coming down," Farkas yelled.

Susie was covering the bag. She was in front of it, waiting for the ball. I had the throw beat. I slid in hard, feet up. I wasn't trying to spike her. But that's how the game is played. I dumped her good. The ball bounced around in the dirt. Pete hadn't backed her up. I got up and took off for third. Ed was playing the bag, waiting for a throw which couldn't possibly be coming. He was faking. Then, all of a sudden, the ball was in Ed's glove. I braked and headed back for second. The girl was there. Ed threw to her. I reversed. They had me in a pickle. Mr. Harmon backed up Ed; Pete finally backed up Susie. I was going to be tagged out, but by whom? I was darned if I'd let her put the tag on me. So I took off for third. She threw to Ed and he put the tag on me as I tried to slip by him.

"Good work all around. Susie, that was a great recovery. That's the way to bounce back."

She was breathing hard, but she was grinning too. At me. I spat.

"OK, I think I've got an idea what you can do in the field, Susie. Now I want to see you hit. Leo, take second. Danny, you'll pitch. Ulmer, you'll bat after Susie. Pick out a bat, young lady."

You'd think Mr. Harmon had just discovered oil. He was grinning. All the girl had done was get up and pick up the ball, which must have hit a stone or something to stay so close to her, and they'd got me out.

It was pure luck, all the way. But she'd need more than luck when she stepped in against my pitches. What I'd done to her in the field was nothing compared to what I was going to do now.

# 9.

MR. HARMON HANDED ME the ball. "All right, Dan, let her hit it."

"You mean that, Mr. Harmon? Don't you want a game situation with her?"

He frowned. "All right, but throw her a few easy ones so she can get her eye back."

I grinned. "You bet."

He went to the first base coaching box, which gave him a pretty good view of Susie Warren, batting right handed.

Susie stepped up to the plate. She was using our skinny brown bat. The lightest bat, of course.

She also choked up on it. Her batting stance was awful. She looked like she was sitting in a chair.

"Stand up and hit like a man," Ed Farkas called down to her.

Sid, grinning, held up his glove. I threw a nice soft pitch up to her. She waited on it, and then she kind of jumped the ball, leaping on it, and hit it into right field for a single.

"C'mon, Danny," Leo said, "she won't get that kind of pitch in a game."

I turned to Leo. I didn't want her to hear it. "Mr. Harmon said throw two easy ones."

Tucker threw the ball in to me on a fly. Sid held up his mitt and I threw another soft one. She jumped this one again and sent a liner out to shortstop. Pete grabbed it and fired to first and George flipped it to me.

Sid squatted. He didn't know the swiftie was coming now. There was no way I could tell him without telling her. But maybe he could tell if I took a little more time and looked in as though I were getting a signal.

Sid got it. He grinned. He nodded.

I went to a full windup and then threw that ball down the middle as hard as I could. It blew by her. She didn't even move her bat. She looked surprised. I winked at her.

"Hey, hey, hey, batter," Leo yelled, "looking good."

"Pretty fat up there, batter."

"No stick, Danny boy," Ed Farkas said.

"Fire it, Dan," Pete called out softly. "Fire it, Dan."

It was a ball game now. It was no longer batting practice. It was a ball game, a tryout under game conditions. Mr. Harmon watched the girl closely.

She stepped out and rubbed some dirt on her hands. She knew it too. She chewed her gum and then stepped in.

Sid wiggled one finger for the fastball and he made his target low. I rocked, kicked, and fired sidearm. A tough pitch on a right-handed batter. But she hung in there. I'll give her credit for that. She hung in there and then chopped at the ball, fouling it off the end of the bat.

"That's a swing," Ed said. "That makes three."

"C'mon, batter, let's hit the ball," Leo called down.

Her hands moved up on the bat. A slow curve, if I could get it over, would be just the thing. She'd be way out in front. Sid saw it too. He wiggled two fingers. I nodded. I gave her the big fastball motion and then bent my curve at her. The ball came right at her. She held her ground, waiting for it to break. I waited too. So did Sid. It didn't break. She ducked at the last second, but not fast enough. The ball bounced off her batting helmet and she fell down.

Mr. Harmon was the first to her after Sid. I should have run in, but I never know what to do when someone gets hurt. Besides, the ball hadn't been thrown that hard.

Mr. Harmon took off her helmet. She sat up. "I'm OK," she said, rubbing her head.

"Take it easy," Mr. Harmon said.

"Danny wasn't trying to hit you," Sid said.

"Of course not," she said, looking out at me.

"Well, I wasn't. If I was trying to hurt you, I would have thrown my fastball."

"Easy," Mr. Harmon said. "No one's accusing you of anything. Now just throw batting practice balls."

"You get thrown at in this league," Leo said. "She's got to get used to that."

"I am," Susie Warren said. She stood up. "I'm OK. I been hit by better pitches than that."

"Hey, hey, hey," Ed Farkas said, grinning.

She put her helmet back on. "Go ahead and throw," she said to me.

"Way to go," Pete said.

Warren McDonald whistled. Tuttle shouted, "Tough, tough, tough."

Sid smiled. "Atta girl," he said.

"Batter up," Mr. Harmon said, smiling.

I felt sheepish. Suddenly I was looking bad. Well, I wouldn't throw her batting practice pitches. I'd take her at her word.

Sid went down in his crouch. He wasn't going to give me a signal. He waited for me to toss a batting practice pitch. I waited for the signal. He looked uneasily down to Mr. Harmon.

"Let's go," Mr. Harmon said.

Nuts to you, Sid, I thought.

I fired the fastball. She got wood on it and sent a grounder down to Leo at second. Leo flipped to George.

"Was that a batting practice pitch?" Mr. Harmon asked me.

"Sure it was," I said lamely.

"That's hitting it, kid," Ed Farkas called down to her.

She blew a bubble and waited.

"Batting practice," Mr. Harmon warned me.

I shrugged. I threw a fat pitch up there and she smacked it over Ed's head into left field.

"Two more," Mr. Harmon said.

She hit the next fat one into right, as though to prove she could hit where she wanted to. And the last pitch, she fooled all of us, doing what I had done. She laid down a bunt. Was she going to try to run me over? I went to field it and looked at her. She was flying down the line. I reached for the ball, but I'd taken my eye off it and it skipped off my glove. I dove for it, but by the time I found the handle she'd made her turn at first and was heading for second.

"Good bunt, Susie," Mr. Harmon called after her as she made her turn at second and headed for third. We watched her round third and head for home. She ran easily; she was as fast as Leo. Leo, I thought, could very possibly be in trouble.

When she crossed the plate, Mr. Harmon came down the line. "We'll get you a uniform tonight, Susie."

And that was that. The tryout was over. George shook her hand and so did Sid, of all people, and the subs came over and shook her hand and then everyone except me and Leo came off the field to shake her hand.

"C'mon, Leo," Pete said, "be a man. She's good."

"I still want to see her hit under real game conditions."

Mr. Harmon laughed. "You will, Leo."

"How about you, Danny?" Pete asked.

I shook my head.

Sid looked at me, surprised. My battery mate. He knew me better than anyone else. He couldn't figure why I didn't want her on the team.

"What's the matter, man?"

I couldn't explain it to him or to any of them.

"Is she going to be on our team, Mr. Harmon?" I asked.

"Yes, she is, Dan," the coach said. "She looked good to me in the field and at the plate. Not many kids would have got a piece of your fast one the way she did. I think she can help the team, don't you?"

The answer was yes, she could help the team. But not as much as I helped the team. What I was going to do now was a gamble. I could lose. But I could also win. It was the only shot I had left. There wasn't anything else I could do.

"Mr. Harmon, if she's going to be on our team, then I'm going to quit."

Everyone stared at me.

"Say that again, Dan."

"If she's gonna be on our team, then I'm going to quit."

"You're kidding," Steinbrunner said.

"Danny, you're acting like a jerk," Farkas said.

"Let me understand this," Mr. Harmon said slowly, and I knew then and there I'd lost my gamble. "You're saying you won't play if she plays."

"If she's on our team, I'm not."

"Why, Dan?"

I swallowed. I couldn't tell them why. They wouldn't understand. None of their folks were divorced. None of them were trying to keep things ready so life could be like it once was. They just wouldn't understand it.

I shook my head.

It made no sense for a coach to trade the best pitcher in the league for a girl second baseman, even if she was good. But that's what Mr. Harmon did.

"I'm sorry to lose you, Dan," he said quietly. "We won't be half as good without you. But if that's the way it has to be . . ."

He waited for me to back out, change my mind.

"That's the way it is," I said.

I got my gear and went home. The practice went on without me.

# 10.

ALL THE WAY HOME I felt like I'd just done a dumb thing. But what else could I have done? Sure, I wanted to play ball more than anything else in the world except for one thing: I wanted to keep Mom set for Dad when he returned. Now I was finished with baseball—for this season—but at least Mom was still set for Dad. Mr. Warren might be going to our games to see Susie play, but he'd go alone because Mom wouldn't go if I wasn't playing.

The way to look at it was like I was injured for the year. Next year I'd switch teams and there'd be no problem. But this year, it was like I was sick and had to stay out a season. Lots of guys got injured and lost a season and it didn't hurt them too much. When Bob Gibson, the St. Louis Cardinal pitcher, was a kid, he was sick a lot and in bed for almost a year and it didn't hurt his fastball too much when he got to the majors. So it would be like I was injured. The important thing was that Mom and Mr. Warren wouldn't have an excuse to see each other.

That made me feel a little bit better by the time I got home. Also Mom wasn't there, which was good because I wasn't ready yet to tell her what I'd just done. It would have to come out naturally.

I went into the kitchen. No meat thawing on the counter. Did that mean we were going out? I opened the freezer. There was hamburger meat in there and some pork chops, along with frozen juice and vegetables. She'd be mad if I thawed out any meat before she got home, but I felt like getting ready for her, helping her with the meal. She usually didn't get home till almost six o'clock, so I had a good half hour almost.

I could scrape some carrots. She likes carrots. So do I. They are supposed to be good for night vision. Most major league games are played at night, so the more carrots I ate now, the better I'd be when I was older.

I got out two carrots and ran cold water over them and was scraping away with a knife when I heard the VW in the driveway. I looked out through the kitchen window. Mom got out of the car with a big bag of groceries. She'd just been to the market a couple of days ago. What was going on? Why was she home so early?

She came up the back steps. I opened the door for her. She was really surprised to see me.

"Why aren't you at practice, Danny?"

"I . . . uh . . . left early." That was the truth.

"Good. You can give me a hand. There're two more bags in the car."

"What's going on?"

"I've invited Herb and his girls for supper."

"What?"

"You heard me. Go get the bags."

"You're kidding."

"I'm not kidding."

"Mom, you didn't."

"What's the matter with you, Danny? Are you going to get those bags in or aren't you?"

"Do they have to come?"

"I'll get them myself."

"I'll get them," I said, and I went down the steps. I thought my stomach was going to fall out. This was awful. I couldn't imagine anything worse than this. I'd quit the team to keep them apart and now the guy was coming here. What was I supposed to do now? Quit the house? And he'd tell her . . . This really was bad.

"Good. Set them down on the counter. Won't it be fun to have a full table? How did Susan's tryout come out?"

My mind was racing along, looking for a way out, but I couldn't find one.

"OK."

"OK for you or OK for her?"

"OK for her."

"That means she made the team."

"Yeah."

Mom laughed. "You don't sound very excited about it."

"I'm not."

I watched her put things away. She looked happy.

"Danny," she said, "you're a male chauvinist pig at the age of eleven. I'd have thought you were a good enough ball player not to be afraid of a girl. Hand me the milk from that bag. Thank you."

"It's not her I'm afraid of."

"And the salami. Thank you."

"It's your friend Herb Warren I'm afraid of."

"Why on earth are you afraid of him?"

I picked up a half-scraped carrot and went on scraping. Here we go, I thought.

" 'Cause I am. 'Cause you like him. 'Cause maybe he likes you. 'Cause I been to his house and it's crummy and this house is nice. 'Cause . . . I don't know. Ain't that enough 'causes?"

"No," Mom said, "it's not even one good 'cause. It's foolishness and you know it."

"I don't know it."

"Yes, you do. You're against Herb Warren and you don't even know him. You don't even want to know him."

"I don't have to know him."

"No, I guess not. As long as you close your mind to everything, you don't have to know anything. Well, I like Herb Warren. I admire Herb Warren. All by himself he's bringing up those girls. He's been a father and mother to them and that's hard work. I know."

"There's one difference, Mom. I got a father."

98

"Not on the premises, Danny."

"What's that mean, 'premises'?"

"It means here, now, when there are problems, when there're worries or joys or anything. Your father's not here."

"He's coming back."

"He's not coming back."

"He is."

"Oh, Danny, how can you be so stubborn? No one's asking you not to be Matt Gargan's boy. But you've got to understand, child, I am not Matt Gargan's wife anymore. And I don't want to be again. Can't you just for once try to look at life from someone else's point of view?"

"No."

She sighed. "You're as stubborn as your father."

"That's right. I'm a ball player like my father. I'm just like my father."

"Not *just* like. But enough like to make you exasperating. Your father wouldn't ever look at things from anyone else's point of view. He had no idea how lonely I was, and you don't either."

"Aw, Mom, you're not that lonely. You got a job. You got me. I'm here."

I looked at her; she looked at me. Suddenly she started to cry. She had an apron on over her nice clothes; there were bags of groceries all over; the refrigerator was half open; and she was crying. What had I said? All I said was that she had me, I was here.

She covered her face with her hands and wept. I felt awful.

"Mom, please stop. I'm sorry. I won't say it again."

"Danny . . ." She was still crying but kind of half laughing too. "Danny, you're sweet and awful all at once. You're right, darling. There's absolutely no reason for you, at the ripe old age of eleven, to see life from my point of view. I'm the one who should apologize. I'd better wash up too. Please don't worry about Herb Warren. We're both making mountains out of molehills. Come on, let's both wash up now. I'd hate for the Warrens to come in now and see you dirty and me full of tears."

We both went to the bathroom and shared the sink. Mom washed off first and then I did. When we were done we looked at ourselves in the mirror. Mom smiled. "I'm sorry for you, Danny. You're getting to look more like me all the time."

"I'm tough. I can take it."

She laughed. "Good. Now change out of your baseball things and then I want you to help me pick up the house. They could be here at any time."

"I bet practice is still going on."

"Why did you leave early, Dan?"

I hesitated. No, now was not the time. Not after her crying like that. The last thing I wanted to do was make her cry again.

"Oh . . . I . . . uh . . . didn't feel so good."

"Did you feel sick?"

"Yeah. A little."

"Where?"

"In my stomach." I had, too, when she told me she'd invited the Warrens over.

"Danny, I'd hate for you not to be at the table to-night. Why don't you change and lie down for a while? There's not much to do here. I can take care of it. If I need you for anything I'll call you. You don't have a fever." She put her hand on my forehead.

"I'm OK," I said.

She kissed me on the forehead. I squirmed but took it.

"And please don't be afraid of anyone or anything. Fear and Danny Gargan don't go together. Now go and lie down."

I went to my room and lay down. Being sick wasn't a bad idea. That way I wouldn't have to be there when Susie Warren tattled on me. She'd probably told her father by now and next she'd tell Mom.

Of course I was just digging a deeper hole for myself, but what else could I do? What would Dad have done? Probably never have got into a jam like this in the first place. But suppose he had? What would he have done? I didn't know. I wished he were here. I'd ask him. But, as Mom said, he wasn't here.

I heard a car coming up the lane. I got off my bed and looked out the window. A blue station wagon was turning into our driveway. Herb Warren was driving it. Sitting next to him was the older daughter. As he pulled up behind the VW, I could see Susie Warren in the backseat. She was still wearing her baseball clothes. Practice must just have ended. He was coming here with the hot news on his tongue, going to tell Mom how I'd quit the team because of Susie.

I lay down on the bed again. I really felt sick now. I probably had a fever too.

Car doors opened and car doors closed. The front doorbell rang.

"Danny," Mom called, "they're here."

I closed my eyes.

The front door opened. Mom greeted him; he greeted her.

"And this is Sallie. Sallie, this is Mrs. Gargan."

I couldn't hear what Sallie said, but Mom said, "Hello, Sallie. I've heard so much about you. And this must be Susie. I hear you did very well. Danny told me you made the team."

If I could have buried myself under my bed I would have done so.

I couldn't hear what Susie said, but a moment later I heard Mom call, "Danny!" And then there came a knock at my door.

"Danny," Mom said.

I pretended I was asleep.

She opened the door. I felt her looking at me.

"Danny Gargan, stop your faking. They're here. I want you to change your clothes."

"I don't feel good."

"You'll feel a lot worse if you're not in the living room in five minutes. So get moving."

I changed my clothes.

The first person I saw in the living room was Susie Warren. She hadn't changed her clothes. She was still in those awful blue jeans and T-shirt and baseball cap with the *B* on it. And, sure enough, she was still chewing bubble gum. Probably the same piece.

"Hello, Dan," Mr. Warren said.

He was standing in the doorway to the kitchen. Smiling. He had me and he knew it.

I felt myself turn red. "Hi," I said, and sat down. It was going to be a long evening.

"I know you know Susie, Dan, but this is my daughter Sallie."

Sallie Warren was tall, thin, and blonde. She had a dress on. Unlike Susie Warren, Sallie Warren looked like a real girl.

"Hi," she said.

"Hi."

"I thought we'd surprise you and give you a ride home from the park, but Susie told me you left early," said Herb Warren.

Was he being funny? I glanced at Susie Warren. She went on chewing her gum, her face, as always, without expression. The two of them were probably going to play cat and mouse with me.

"Yeah," I said, "I left early."

Mom came into the living room. She had taken her apron off. She looked pretty. "Dinner will be ready in a few minutes. Sallie, Susie, Danny, would you like some pop?"

"I'm fine, Mrs. Gargan," Sallie Warren said politely.

"How about you, Susie?"

"I'm thirsty," Susie Warren said.

"That's no way to answer," Mr. Warren said.

"When someone asks you if you want pop and you do, you say, 'Yes, thank you.'"

Susie Warren shrugged and said, "Yes, thank you."

Mom laughed. "Danny," she said to me, "would you get Susie some pop and get some for yourself too? Carbonated pop can be good for an upset stomach. Danny's not feeling too well," Mom explained to them. "That's why he left practice early."

I winced and waited for the correction to come, but it didn't.

"Oh, what's the matter?" Mr. Warren asked.

"I'm OK now," I said, and went into the kitchen. I'd have liked to keep going out of the kitchen and out of the house, but the pop was alongside the refrigerator.

"He almost never gets sick when he's playing ball. That's why I was a little worried for a while. But I think he's OK. And I understand you did very well, Susie."

"That's right," Mr. Warren said proudly. "By the time I got there, she'd made the team. The coach told me she looked pretty good at second base."

"My sister, the jock," Sallie Warren said.

"I'd rather be a jock than a painter," Susie said.

"You don't have any choice, do you?" her sister said.

"I can paint."

"Badly."

"Who says?"

"I say."

I came back into the living room with Susie Warren's pop, in a glass with ice. She was too busy glaring at her sister to notice it.

"Here," I said. She took the glass without looking at me.

Mr. Warren laughed at the girls. He said that when he was young he used to go back and forth between books and ball. Now he had one girl who was an artist and one girl who was a ball player. "I guess this is called the age of specialization. What do you do when you're not playing ball, Dan?"

"Watch ball games."

"And when you're not doing that?"

"I listen to them on the radio."

Mr. Warren grinned. "And when you're not doing that?"

"I'm eating or sleeping."

"And it's very embarrassing," Mom said, "but speaking about eating, I think we're ready to eat. As soon as Susie finishes her pop, Danny, would you show her where to wash up?"

"I'm finished," Susie said. She drank it down in one gulp, the way I did and Pete and Leo and Sid did when we were thirsty.

"C'mon," I said.

She followed me into the hall. "There's the bathroom," I said.

"Thanks."

"What'd your dad say when you told him I quit the team?"

"I didn't tell him."

"Why not?"

She shrugged. "I don't know."

I felt better, but I didn't let her see that. "How'd practice go after I left?"

"OK."

"Are the guys sore at me?"

"They think you'll change your mind and play tomorrow."

"I won't. Is Mr. Harmon sore?"

"I don't know."

"I think he is. He's a pretty strict coach. Are you gonna tell my mom I quit?"

She looked at me. "Do you want me to?"

I shrugged, but I heard myself say, "No."

"Then I won't."

"I'll tell her myself later. There's soap on the side there."

"Yeah. Thanks. I see it."

She shut the door and a second later I heard her washing up. She wasn't all bad, for a girl.

# 11.

I HAVE TO ADMIT that for a while it was a kind of fun dinner. Mr. Warren told stories about funny things that happened to them in Ohio and Sallie would correct him and then Susie would correct her and the three of them would argue about what had really happened. Mom and I just listened.

But then there came some awkward moments. Mr. Warren asked me where the game was tomorrow and I told him it was over at Vets and he wanted to know where Vets was. When I showed him on a map, he saw that Rawson Junior High was on his way to the game and he asked Mom if she'd like him to pick her up.

My eyes met Susie's. But she didn't say anything, and I couldn't.

Mom said, "Why, I think that would be fine."

"Good. What time do the games start, Dan?"

I hesitated. Now was the time to tell Mom and him, tell them there was no point in her going to the game.

But I couldn't say it.

"Five thirty," I heard myself say.

"Let's say I drop by the library a little after five."

"I'll wait outside," Mom said, "so you won't have to park."

"You don't have to. I can."

And on the two of them went. I avoided Susie Warren's eyes. It was crazy. The whole purpose of my quitting the team was so they wouldn't go to games together and here they were, planning to go together. I'd tell Mom alone. I'd wait till the Warrens went and then I'd be able to tell Mom alone. And then she could telephone him and tell him she wouldn't be going.

After dinner Mom offered everyone a tour of her garden.

"I'm no gardener," Mr. Warren said. "They all look like petunias to me. Danny and I will get a running start on the dishes."

"You'll do no such thing, Herb. We have a dishwasher. It takes me five minutes to put things away. With a running start I'll be a half hour behind."

Herb Warren laughed. "Not with our kind of running start. Go on and check out the flowers, girls."

"Oh, Daddy," Sallie Warren said. And then she said to Mom as they went out, "Daddy doesn't know one flower from another, but he means well . . ."

"I take it you're not big on gardening either," Herb Warren said to me.

"No," I said. I had to be careful with him. I could see he was trying to buddy up to me.

"My wife used to try to get me interested in flowers, but I found it hard. Where's the bread go, Dan?"

"I'll put it away." The last thing I wanted was him knowing where everything went. He was making himself right at home. And who could blame him? East Baker Place was a crummy place to live; this was a nice place.

He watched me put things away. You could see him figuring everything out. This guy moved fast.

So I stopped putting things away and began rinsing the dishes off before putting them into the dishwasher.

He said, "If I could only get my girls interested in doing dishes. You know what they say? They say washing dishes is boring."

He laughed. I did too before I could stop. He did have a good sense of humor.

"How did Susan look to you on the diamond?"

Careful now, I thought.

"Good."

"I hope nobody made it easy for her."

Was he setting a trap? Had he heard about my bumping her around and hitting her with a pitch? But his face was serious. Play the ball, I thought. Don't let it play you.

"Nope. No one made it easy."

"Good. I like it that way and I know Susie does too. I'm not crazy about her playing on boys' baseball teams. There really are physical differences between boys and girls that can make sports unequal. But she loves hardball and there are no girls' hardball teams, and I don't see why she shouldn't have the chance to play. Do you?"

"Nope."

"Is this a good team you play tomorrow?"

I suspected a trap. He was leading up to something. Did he know I'd quit? Susie said she hadn't told him, but maybe someone else had. Mr. Harmon?

"Yeah. They finished second to us last year."

"It should be a good game then?"

"Yeah."

He smiled. "Your mom's a real fan. She loves watching you play, she told me."

He did know. He wouldn't have said that if he didn't know. Susie had lied to me. She *had* told him. I hesitated. Play it carefully, Gargan. He's not giving anything away. Don't you either.

"My dad taught her a lot about baseball," I said. It was a good counterpunch. It got him away from me and reminded him I had a father. And a heck of a father!

"I'd imagine he did. How often do you see your dad, Dan?"

"Three or four times a year. Mostly in the winter. I go to Chicago. We have real good times there."

"I'm sure you do."

"I figure to see more of him next year."

**110**

"How's that?"

"This'll probably be his last season. Then he's gonna retire."

"Is that right?"

"Yep. And move here."

"I didn't know that."

"Not many people do."

"Did your dad tell you that?"

"He doesn't have to. I can tell. He's from Arborville. He wants to come back here. He could get any job in town he wanted. He could run for mayor. My dad's the most famous person ever to come out of Arborville."

"I bet he is. And you're proud of him too, aren't you?"

"You bet I am. He's the first Arborville boy ever to make the major leagues, and I'm going to be the second."

"I hope so. I wish you luck, Dan."

"It's more than luck. It's hard work and playing a lot of ball. That's what Dad says. When he comes back home next year, I'm hoping he'll coach our team."

"What about Mr. Harmon?"

"He'd be tickled to have Dad coach."

"Did he tell you that?"

"No, but I know it."

Mr. Warren looked at me a moment and then he smiled. "Well, Dan, it sounds like everything is going your way."

"It sure is," I said cheerfully.

The back door opened and Mom came into the

kitchen followed by the girls. "Come on, you two. Out of the kitchen."

"We were just talking," Mr. Warren protested.

"We can all talk in the living room."

Mom shooed us out. She and the girls came with us.

"Well, how were the flowers?" Mr. Warren asked his daughters.

"Mrs. Gargan has a real nice garden, Dad," Sallie said. "I wish we had a garden like that."

"You can have one. You get Mrs. Gargan to teach you about flowers and I'll buy the fertilizer."

Mom laughed. "Herb, I think you ought to tell Danny about some of the books you've written."

"Oh, no," Sallie groaned.

"No, tell him, Dad," Susie said.

"Danny's never met a real live author before," Mom said.

"Not an author," Herb Warren said. "I'll be an author when I get published. Right now I'm just a librarian who gets up early in the morning to write and writes late at night before he goes to bed. Speaking of which, it really is time to be going."

"Do we have to go already?" Susie Warren asked. I looked at her, surprised. All she did was sit and chew bubble gum, and now she was pretending she was having a good time.

"I'm afraid so. It's almost ten o'clock. Nancy, it's really been a treat for me and the girls."

"Herb, it's been a treat for Dan and me. Usually we eat quietly and mumble a few words and watch TV."

112

"We talk," I protested.

Mom smiled. "Sometimes. But I can't remember when I've heard so much commotion at our table. We'll do it again. Good night, Sallie."

"Good night, Mrs. Gargan. And thanks a lot. It was a swell meal. And thanks for showing us the garden. You've got swell flowers. Good night, Danny."

"Yeah. G'night."

"Good night, Susie. And congratulations on making the baseball team."

Susie Warren blushed. Mr. Warren and Sallie laughed.

"Good night," she mumbled. And she turned to me and nodded.

I nodded to her.

"Nancy," Mr. Warren said, holding out his hand, "I'll pick you up tomorrow in front of Rawson around five."

Mom shook his hand. "I'll be ready. It'll be fun watching the two of them."

Susie Warren and I looked at each other. I looked away.

"It certainly will," Herb Warren said. Susie hadn't lied. He didn't know. It was me who was going to have to tell Mom and break this thing up once and for all.

"Good night, Dan," he said to me. "See you tomorrow."

"G'night," I said.

They left and Mom went out behind them. "Come on, Dan. We'll see them to their car."

Which meant more good-byes at the car. Finally they got their car backed out of our driveway and Mom waved till they were out of sight around the corner. You'd have thought they were leaving for China.

Mom put her hand on my shoulder and squeezed it. She was happy. "Wasn't that fun?"

"It was OK."

"Aren't they a nice family?"

"Yeah. Listen, Mom, I got to tell you something."

"They're more than nice. I think that Sallie Warren is beautiful, don't you?"

"Sure. Listen, Mom. About tomorrow . . ."

"And I think Susie is adorable. And what a good sport she is."

"Yeah. Listen, Mom, about tomorrow. The game . . ."

"Yes? What about it?"

I cleared my throat. "There's no point in your going."

That stopped her. "What did you say?"

"I said, 'There's no point in your going.' "

"Why not?"

" 'Cause I won't be there. I quit the team."

She stared at me.

"Are you serious?"

"Yes."

"When did you do that?"

"Today. That's why I came home early. I wasn't sick. I . . . lied about that. I quit."

"But why did you do that, Dan? You love that team. You love baseball."

**114**

There was only one way to say it, and that was to come out and say it.

"I quit 'cause when she made the team I knew he'd start coming to games with you. And . . ."

She understood. She looked at me, and for a moment I thought she was going to cry again. But she didn't.

"I see," she said. Her mouth got tough. "I understand it all now. Well, Danny Gargan, a gentleman asked me to go to a baseball game with him tomorrow and I'm going, whether you're there or not."

And with that she turned her back on me and went inside the house. A moment later I heard the sounds of dishes being put in the dishwasher . . . hard.

"If you go to the game," I shouted up through the kitchen window, "and I'm not there, everyone will know you're chasing that guy."

"You go jump in the lake, Danny Gargan," Mom shouted back down at me.

"They'll know there's no reason for you to go to a ball game when your son isn't playing."

She slammed the window shut.

The battle lines were drawn. And it didn't look good for me. If she went and I didn't play, I'd have lost—and we both knew it.

Now what, Danny Gargan?

# 12.

YOU GOT NO PROBLEMS when you sleep. So I forced myself to sleep late, which meant till after Mom went off to work. That meant we didn't have to argue.

When I got down to the kitchen around eight thirty, there was a note from her telling me to have juice, cereal, milk, and toast. And reminding me that Mrs. King expected me to do her lawn before this weekend. I'd forgotten about that. I'm not a great chore man. There are kids who're always earning extra money; I'm not one of them. I'll earn the big money playing ball. These kids may grow up to be professional lawn mowers or snow shovelers or leaf rakers; I'll be a professional baseball player.

But Mrs. King and Mom were friends and she's

old, so I agreed to cut her grass. After eating breakfast and washing the dishes, I went over to Mrs. King's house on Hermitage Street, which is just a couple of blocks from us, got her old push mower out of her garage, and cut her grass. It was hard going because the lawn was bumpy, but I didn't mind. For one thing, it got me out of the house. Now that Mom was safely off to work, the only thing I had to worry about was the guys coming around to bug me. I needed peace and quiet while I tried figuring this whole mess out.

I didn't get it.

"Hey, man," a voice called out. It was Sid Grayson, my catcher. He was riding his sister's bicycle and he looked big on it.

He biked up to where I was pushing the mower. "I been looking for you," he said.

"Yeah?"

"Yeah. What gives? We got a game today. Are you still quit?"

"Yeah."

"C'mon, Danny. Change your mind."

"No way."

"Just 'cause a girl's gonna play with us?"

"It's not that."

"What is it then?"

I had no answer for him 'cause the answer didn't make sense to me anymore. I'd quit so Mom and this guy wouldn't go to games together and now she was going anyway.

"I don't want to talk about it, Sid."

"Has it got to do with Mr. Harmon?"

"No."

"Me?"

" 'Course not. None of you guys."

"None of us, not the coach, not the girl . . . what's it about?"

"Sid, forget it."

"Yeah. But how? We'll lose if you don't pitch today."

"You won't lose."

"Yes, we will. Lou'll keep 'em off base for two innings. Then those guys'll start timing his curve."

"You pitch then." Sid had a great arm.

"Who'll catch? The girl?"

I laughed. "I may come and watch that."

"If you come, Danny, you play. I'll pick you up and set you down on the mound."

Sid could do it too.

"I won't come then."

"Danny, this'll be the first game we've lost in three years. The guys'll be sore at you."

"I know."

"I'll be sore at you. In fact, I'm sore at you right now."

"Sid, I got to cut this grass."

He looked at me and then he gave up. "Come on over to the park after lunch. We're gonna be shooting baskets."

"Maybe."

"You gonna quit shooting baskets too?"

"No. I'll see."

"See you later," Sid said.

"Yeah. See you, Sid."

I watched him ride off on his sister's bike: a big,

square, solid, dependable guy. He'd never quit. At least, not without a good reason. Well, I had a good reason when I quit, but it wasn't good anymore. Or was it? What had changed? Nothing had changed yet. I still had to fight to keep things as they were for Dad.

The White Sox were on TV tonight against the Brewers. Dad was probably out at the park right now practicing. Then they'd have the afternoon off. I could probably reach Dad about five o'clock our time. He'd be home in his little apartment, cooking himself up a small steak. I could call him and talk this whole thing over with him. I could let him know what I'd done and ask him what he thought I ought to do next. I needed advice and he was the only one who could give it to me.

The moment that came clear to me, I felt a lot better. Mrs. King's lawn didn't feel so bumpy either.

The rest of the day I avoided Sampson Park. The guys were the last people I wanted to see. I biked down to Ferry Field and watched the university trackmen work out. Then I biked over to the university golf course and watched people tee off. Golf looked like a dumb game. Hit a ball and walk a mile and hit it again and walk another mile. Golfers were almost as out of shape as softball players. Those were two sports I'd never play, golf and softball.

I went home around three o'clock and made myself a couple of salami sandwiches and had two glasses of chocolate milk. Then I watched daytime quiz shows on TV until it was five. Then I set about calling Chicago on the phone. Mom was good about letting me call Dad. She once told me I could call him anytime I wanted to. Dad didn't call here as much as he once did. I guess it was kind of embarrassing for him when Mom answered the phone. They were sort of polite with each other, and then Mom got me and he and I talked about all kinds of things.

I got Dad's number out of the back of the phone book. Then I dialed 1 and then the area code, 312, and then his number. He was probably in his kitchen now. It'd take him a couple of minutes to get to the phone.

It didn't take more than two rings before the phone was picked up. To my surprise, a woman said hello.

Wrong number, I thought. Now what do I do on a long-distance call? I just lost us a lot of money.

"Hello," the woman said again.

"I guess I got the wrong number," I said.

"What number did you want?"

I gave her Dad's number.

"This is it," she said.

"Oh. Is . . . Matt Gargan there?"

"Yes, he is. Can I tell him who's calling?"

"His son—Danny Gargan."

"Danny? I thought it might be you. How happy he'll be. One moment, Danny. Matt," she called. "Matt, it's for you. It's your son Danny. He'll be right here, Danny."

She seemed to know me. She seemed to know all about me. I didn't know anything about her.

"It's Danny," she repeated, her voice away from the phone now.

"Dan," Dad said, "how are you?"

"I'm fine," I said slowly. "How are you?"

"Great. We won last night in the eleventh inning."

"How did you do?" I asked.

"I got in in the eighth and drew a walk. Can you imagine putting an old man like me on base and making him run?"

I heard the woman laugh. Who was she?

"How's your team doing? Where're you calling from? Home?"

"Yeah. The team's OK. I just called to . . . say hello."

"Well, son, I'm glad you did. I want you to meet someone very dear to me, Danny. I was going to bring you out to Chicago in a couple of weeks to have you meet her, but you might as well meet her by phone. Ruth, get on the other phone, would you? Danny, the person who answered the phone is . . . well . . . Ruth and I are going to get married as soon as the season is over." I heard the other phone being lifted off the receiver. "Are you there, Ruth?"

"Yes, Matt," the woman said.

"Ruth, I'd like you to meet my son Danny. You've heard me talk about him."

"I've heard him talk about no one else, Danny," the woman named Ruth said. "How are you?"

"Fine," I said. I didn't know what else to say. I could hardly even hear myself say that.

"Danny, hang up and let me call you back," Dad said. "This is going to be a long call and your mom might get upset."

"No, she won't," I said. "It's OK."

121

"Well, son, you and Ruth are going to get along fine. She's got two children of her own, a boy named Tom and a girl named Kim, and we're going to be one big family when we get together, won't we, Ruth?"

The woman named Ruth laughed. "I guess so."

"Tom's nine, Dan. And Kim is seven. You'll like them both. Tom knows you're a terrific ball player. I've told him all about your team. You and Sid and Pete. When I get you out here you'll have to show him some things about pitching. I told him I tried to turn you into a catcher, but your big talent is striking people out."

The woman named Ruth laughed again. Dad laughed too. I guess I laughed. I heard myself laugh.

"Matt," Ruth said, "I'm going to get off the line and let you two chat. It's nice to meet you, Danny, even over the phone. I hope I get to see you real soon."

"You will," Dad said.

"Bye-bye, Danny."

"Bye," I said.

The phone went click.

There was a silence. Dad and I were alone. I heard him clear his throat. "Well, Danny, kind of a surprise, huh?"

"Yeah."

"I've known Ruth almost a year now. She's divorced too. She's a fine person. We're pretty suited to each other. She loves baseball. Her father was a semipro ball player. We knew pretty well right away, but we wanted to give ourselves time. I guess the time's up now. I should have called you, or written, but . . ."

He paused.

". . . but I wanted to be sure, and I . . . didn't want to . . . hurt your mom. How is she, Dan?"

"She's great," I said. "She's really doing swell. She loves her job and she's got a guy, Dad. A really nice guy. His name's Herb Warren. He's the coordinator of libraries and he's a widower—his wife died, and he's got two kids too. A girl named Sallie who's a terrific painter and a girl named Susie who's a ball player. Isn't that the nuts, Dad? A girl being a ball player."

"Any good?" Dad asked.

"She made our team." I laughed. "Isn't that crazy? If Mom and Herb Warren get married, I'll have a sister playing second base."

Dad laughed. I laughed too. Dad said, "Danny, it sounds like things are working out well for everyone. I'm happy for your mom."

"So am I."

"I'll write you as soon as we set a date for the wedding and I'll send you plane fare. Will you come?"

"Sure I'll come, Dad. If I'm going to Mom's wedding, I might as well go to yours."

Dad laughed again and so did I. Then he said some more things about everyone being happy and everything coming up roses and I said they sure were and then he hung up and I hung up and I burst into tears. Right then and there. Looking at the darn telephone, I burst into tears and cried like a baby.

I don't know how long I cried, but after a while I got all cried out. Like there were no more tears inside and it was stupid to go on crying. So I went into the bathroom and washed up and looked at myself in the mirror.

Baby, I said to myself. You're a darn baby. You sit around like a goofball making plans, and when they don't work out 'cause they're stupid to start with, you start crying.

I scrubbed my face with my washcloth. Then I went and got my uniform. It had been tough talking to Dad, listening to his "good news," but the toughest part of the day was yet to come.

# 13.

MR. HARMON AND MRS. TUTTLE AND MRS. GRAYSON usually give rides to "away" games from the Sampson Park parking lot. The cars leave around four thirty. Games are at five thirty. It was practically five thirty by the time I finished talking with Dad. Our game against Harts was at Vets Park, which was all the way across town. By the time I got my uniform on it was twenty to six, and by the time I got to Vets Park on my bike it was six o'clock.

It would be a lot harder rejoining the team than quitting it. Just to start with, I was a half hour late. Mr. Harmon never let anyone who was two minutes late get into a game. Still, what did I have to lose? I'd have to take some nasty remarks and keep my mouth shut and hope Mr. Harmon wasn't too sore at me to let me back on the team.

I pedaled as hard as I could, going across the university campus, and then going the wrong way on one-way streets because I was following the shortest route there. I went down Liberty to First Street and then against the traffic on First to Washington and then to Huron and then uphill on Huron all the way to Vets. I was one tired ball player by the time I reached Vets Park. Then I had to ride across the park because the guys were playing on Diamond No. 5 all the way at the other end.

I cut across the outfields of two other baseball games and people shouted at me to get off the field.

"I'm getting," I grunted, and kept pedaling as hard as I could.

I came up to Diamond No. 5 and cut to the first base side where our bench was. We were out in the field. Harts had runners on first and second. Lou Salmon was pitching. I looked at second base. Leo was there. Pete was at short. Farkas was on third. I looked at the stands behind third base, and sure enough there were Mom and Herb Warren. I couldn't tell whether they saw me or not. It didn't make any difference. I hadn't come because of them. I'd come because this was where I belonged, this was where my life was. I'd been a dope to fool around with the things that meant the most to me.

I pedaled over to our bench and got off the bike behind it. I got the royal welcome of the year— complete silence. Everyone ignored me. Harts had two men on.

I knocked my kickstand down and sat down beside Simple Ulmer.

"What's the score?"

Simple looked at me. "Where've you been? I thought you quit."

"What's the score?"

"3–1, them. They got two men on."

"I know."

"Danny's here, Mr. Harmon," one of the other subs said.

Mr. Harmon ignored him and ignored me. I winced. I was in for it now. Well, I deserved it. I saw Leo look at me, and Pete too. Pete nodded. I knew he was glad I'd shown up, anyway. Pete wants to win.

I looked down our bench past Mr. Harmon. Susie Warren was sitting at the far end, snapping her bubble gum. While I watched, she cupped her hands to her mouth and hollered, "He can't hit, Lou. He's no hitter."

I grinned, got up, and walked behind the bench, giving Mr. Harmon a wide berth. He knew I was there. The only way I'd get in the game was to let him find me. It wouldn't do me any good to "find" him.

"Can I sit down?" I asked her.

She looked up, startled. "Huh? Oh." She moved over.

Lou threw a strike.

"What's the count?"

"Two and one. One out."

"How'd those guys get on?"

"Hits. They're good hitters," she said as though it was unusual.

"Sure they are," I said. "They finished second to us last year. You're not in Ohio now."

She snapped her gum at me.

"C'mon, Lou," I yelled. "Blow it by him."

Lou glanced over at me. He grinned. I grinned back at him and made a fist to let him know I was behind him. He didn't have to do it all himself.

I thought he put out a little extra on the next pitch. He kicked a little higher as he poured his fast one over. The guy popped it up to second. Leo called for it and took it in. Two outs. Men on first and second.

"Way to chuck," Mr. Harmon called out, and marked his scorecard.

Our infield talked up. The outfield was noisy too. Sid held up his index finger and pinky. "Two away," he shouted. "Play at any base. Two outs."

"Hey, Danny," Charley Campbell said. "You back on the team?"

He said it purposely loud enough for Mr. Harmon to hear. I replied loud enough for Mr. Harmon to hear too. "I sure hope so."

"Me too," Charley said.

Lou Salmon slipped a strike over, then a ball, then the batter hit a hard ground ball down to third. Ed Farkas had to back up to field it, which meant he only had a play at first. But he made it, and the side was out. Our bench cheered. The guys came running in.

"Hello, Danny," Sid Grayson said, grinning from ear to ear.

"Hello, man."

"Gargan's here, Pete," Simple said.

"I see him."

"Hey, man, glad to see you."

"Danny, boy, how's the arm?"

"Gargan, you still got a uniform, huh?"

The guys weren't making any big thing out of it, but I could tell they were glad I was back. They kind of nudged me with their gloves. Pete winked at me. Leo swatted at my head. Joe Tuttle stopped right in front of me. "You look familiar, fella," he said.

I laughed. So did the other guys. It wasn't as hard as I'd thought it would be. Only Mr. Harmon hadn't greeted me. Lou came over.

"Move over," I said to Susie. She squeezed. So did I. "How's it going?"

"Better, now that you're here. I kept thinking I'd have to pitch five or six innings and I wasn't working hard enough. I'll work harder now."

I was going to say, "Better not. Mr. Harmon hasn't said a thing to me," but I didn't. You should work as hard as you can. Dad used to say there's more pitches in your arm than you think if your head is willing. And then, Mr. Harmon might play me. And heck, we were losing. There's no point in slacking off when you're behind.

"What inning is it?"

"Top of the third. You see their faces when they saw you?"

"Nope."

"Kittleson almost fell off the bench. They heard you quit. Hey, Danny, have you?"

"I'd like to get back."

"Mr. Harmon say anything?"

"Not yet. You keep chucking hard. How're you pitching Kittleson?"

"Tight."

"Good. What about Marcheski?"

"Low balls. Sid and I went over the lineup. Now we got to get some hits. I can hold 'em now that I know you're here."

"Grayson, Steinbrunner, Farkas, Tuttle," Mr. Harmon said. "Let's get some hits, boys. We need base runners."

"Danny's here, Dad," Tucker Harmon said.

Mr. Harmon ignored him. "Sid," he said, putting his arm around our catcher, "don't be anxious up there. Kittleson throws them slower than it looks. Just let your bat do the work."

Sid nodded. Mr. Harmon went off to coach third base. Sid swung the weighted bat and then threw it away. Tucker came over to me. "How're you, Danny?"

"OK."

"I tried to tell Dad you were here."

"He knows it, Tuck. Leave it alone."

"Sure. But we could use you, your bat too."

"You guys are only two runs behind. Let's talk it up."

"Give it a ride, Sid," Susie Warren hollered.

"Hey, Kittleson, your ears stick out."

"Blast it out, Sid."

"Kittleson, wipe your nose before you pitch."

Kittleson was a pretty good pitcher though, and

he didn't rattle easy. Susie yelled and I yelled and so did the whole bench. I wondered if they were up this much before I got there. But I wasn't going to ask.

Behind third base, four rows up, Mom and Herb Warren were sitting together. I wondered how I was going to tell her about the phone call. I would. To-night. I'd have to. There'd be a big bill on that phone call.

"Talk it up, Danny," Susie Warren said, jabbing me in the side. I grinned. She was OK.

"Hey, pitcherpitcherpitcher," I hollered.

Sid was first-ball hitting. Too anxious. He wanted to hit a home run. All we wanted was men on base. Way out ahead, he poled a long foul fly ball down the left field line. It was an easy out for their left fielder.

"Take your time on those pitches," Pete said. "He gives us a big motion, but there's no steam there."

"We need a base runner, George," Mr. Harmon called down to Steinbrunner. Big George dug his spikes into the dirt. Like Sid, he swung from the bottom of the bat. Like Sid, he was greedy. He couldn't wait. He, too, lifted a long, high fly ball to left field. An easy out. The guys were ahead of the pitches, trying to kill the ball.

"Ed," Pete said softly to Ed Farkas, "lay it down."

"Are you kidding? I can hit this guy in my sleep."

"Better close your eyes then," McDonald said.

"We need a runner. Lay it down," Pete said.

"Nuts," Farkas said. He was the biggest pull hitter on our team. Everyone knew it, including the other team. Their third baseman moved over and played the foul line; so did the left fielder. The shortstop moved into the hole between third and short; the second baseman moved to the third base side of second. All Ed had to do was lay a bunt down the first base line. The second baseman would never get over. But Ed was thick in the head. A pull hitter is often a great hitter, and a great hitter usually wears blinders and does his thing, no matter how they're playing him.

Ed did his thing. He pulled a wicked line drive right into the third baseman's hands and we were out. We should have been leading those guys by five runs instead of being behind by two.

Mr. Harmon came back to the bench shaking his head. I looked at him, hoping to catch his eye, but I couldn't. He hadn't said hello, and I had the sinking feeling he wouldn't say hello.

"Three up and three down, Lou," Susie Warren called out to Salmon. "Up they come and down they go."

She was a good sport, I thought. If she was unhappy about "playing the bench," she didn't show it.

"Picking cherries," she hollered.

"What's that mean?" I asked her.

She blew a bubble. "I don't know. We used to say that in Ohio. Sometimes we said picking peaches."

I laughed. She frowned, and then she clapped her hands and hollered, "C'mon, you guys. No mistakes. Shoot that ball . . ." She was a real talker-upper. I had the feeling Mr. Harmon was looking our way and studying her. Maybe it was me he was looking at; I couldn't tell.

With the guys in the field, our bench was three-quarters empty. It would have been easy for Mr. Harmon to ask me to come over, ask me if I'd changed my mind, but he was ignoring me. Well, that was right. Fair. I'd asked for it. If I couldn't play, I'd talk it up for the guys. He hadn't told me to leave the bench. That meant something, didn't it?

"No batter, Lou," I yelled. "No batter there."

Lou looked cool and poised out there. He had a natural curveball and he was always around the plate. He got the first man on a grounder to George at first. The second guy dumped a single over Ed's head. The third guy popped out, and the fourth guy struck out.

We were in again. And this time we were smarter with our bats. Joe Tuttle, batting seventh, dropped the bunt Farkas should have dropped, and he beat the throw from the catcher. He stole second on the next pitch. That shook up Kittleson and he walked Warren McDonald. Tucker Harmon was up with two men on and nobody out. His dad came down the line and talked to him. Tucker nodded. Then Mr. Harmon flashed the bunt sign to Joe and Warren. Mr. Harmon was playing for those two runs on bases. He wanted them both in scoring position.

Tucker took a couple of high pitches and then he dropped a nice bunt down. Kittleson came off the mound to field it. He picked it up and turned to fire to third. But Joe Tuttle was in already. So he whirled and fired to first. His throw was high; it sailed past first base. Joe came home, Warren took third, and Tucker went on to second.

Our bench was yelling. The score 3–2, no one out, men on second and third, and the top of the lineup coming up.

Pete stepped in.

"He got a double in the first inning," Susie Warren said, reading my mind.

"How'd Leo do in the first inning?" I asked.

If she was going to get in the game, it would be at Leo's position.

"He got a hit," she said. "He's a good hitter too."

"Give it a ripple, Pete," I yelled.

Pete took a couple of practice swings and then stepped in. He could hit with a choked bat or a long bat. He could hit to all fields. He had good eyes and good wrists.

They had a meeting at the mound, trying to figure out how to play this. Finally they decided to bring the infield in and try to keep the runner at third. Pete watched them. Then he took a "swing away" sign from Mr. Harmon.

Kittleson threw up his medium fastball, which was always so tempting to try to kill. Pete resisted the temptation, and at the last second crossed up everyone by dropping the third bunt in a row in that inning. Kittleson raced in without looking at Mc-Donald, who was on third, scooped up the ball, and tossed it to his catcher. The only trouble was that no one was going. McDonald wasn't forced. He stayed right there on third. Tucker stayed on second and Pete scooted across first base.

Bases were loaded.

"Chance to be a hero, Reilly," I said.

Leo grinned at me. "About time too."

"Bring those ducks home, Reilly," Susie Warren said.

Leo looked at her and shook his head. "Too much," he said. "Too much."

"What's the matter with him?" Susie asked.

"What's this duck thing?"

"That's what we said in Ohio."

"Man, you're not there now."

She grinned. "Right. Bring them home, Reilly. Bring them home."

"Would he have made your team in Ohio?"

"You all would have made it," she said.

"Where would that have put you?"

She blew a bubble at me, snapped it, turned, and hollered, "C'mon, bust 'em up, Reilly."

Leo stepped in. Their infield was playing in tight. They had to try to cut off the tying run at the plate. Leo was a good punch hitter. He could punch a ball right through that tightly drawn-in infield. If he waited for the right pitch.

The first pitch was a ball. Then Kittleson threw a nice curve for a strike. Leo fouled off a fastball. Then Kittleson tried to jam him with another fastball. Leo stepped back. With the count two and two, Kittleson, not wanting to go to three and two, threw a fast one down the middle. It was a mistake. Leo

135

timed it and smacked it through the tightly drawn-in infield for a single.

Warren McDonald scored. Tucker scored. Pete took third on the throw home and Leo took second. We were ahead 4–3.

I looked at the stands. Mom was clapping her hands, the way women do at ball games, as though they were concerts. Herb Warren was sitting there watching quietly, the way ex–ball players do when they're really interested in what's going on.

Lou Salmon batted next. I was surprised to see him batting third. That was my number when I started a game. When Lou started, Mr. Harmon batted him ninth, but when he came in for me in games, he batted in my spot, of course. Now he was starting and batting third. He wasn't a good hitter. He slapped at the ball. Usually he made contact, but he never sent it very far and he wasn't fast getting down the line.

He took a couple of bad pitches and then slapped a soft liner to the third baseman for an easy out. Everyone held on base.

That brought Sid up with one out and Pete and Reilly at third and second. This time Sid waited on the fat pitch. He waited and waited and when it came he slugged it out into left center. It was ticketed home run all the way. A three-run homer. And that gave us a 7–3 lead.

"I need all the runs I can get," Lou confided to me.

We all met Sid at home plate. Susie Warren was just about the first to shake his hand. I could see

Mrs. Grayson in the stands beaming, accepting congratulations from Mom and Herb Warren.

That finished Kittleson and finished Harts Trucks too. They brought in their big first baseman Arch White to pitch. He was strong and could get the ball over. But it was like facing a pitching machine that had only one speed. After a while you caught on to it. George took a couple of pitches and then drilled a single into right field. Ed forced him at second with a bouncer to shortstop. Joe Tuttle, batting for the second time in the inning, laid down a surprise bunt that moved Ed to second and beat it out himself. With men on first and second, McDonald popped up and finally we were out of the inning.

"You got a big cushion," I said to Lou. "All you got to do is let them pop it up."

"Sure. But stick around just the same."

"I'm not going anywhere."

Mr. Harmon came back to the bench all smiles for everyone but me. "Ulmer, Campbell, Warren . . . I'm going to get you in the game in the fifth inning."

Simple Ulmer looked at me. So did Charley Campbell. But Mr. Harmon didn't. Out on the mound, Lou Salmon went to work.

He got them out one-two-three, working like a surgeon—brisk, businesslike, confident. Still, I didn't think Mr. Harmon would pitch him all seven innings. That would mean Lou would have no eligibility left for the next game. If he wouldn't let me play, then Pete would pitch. Mr. Harmon would move Reilly to shortstop and put Susie Warren at second.

137

And that's exactly what he did in the fifth inning. He put Pete on the mound, moved Leo to shortstop, and put Susie Warren on second. And then disaster struck.

# 14.

"HEY, GONZALEZ," someone on their bench shouted, "don't turn around, but you got a girl playing second."

"She's real cute, Pete. Is she your girl or Reilly's?"

"She's pretty enough to play catcher."

"She's got nice form, Pete."

Pete ignored the jeers as he took the last of his warmup tosses. If Susie Warren heard the shouts, she didn't show it. She took the throw down to second from Sid and then tossed the ball to Leo, and around the infield the ball went.

The razzing went on.

"Hey, Pete, did you find her in dancing school?"

"How long you guys been playing with girls?"

Pete looked in and took his sign from Sid. Pete's no pitcher; he's a ball player with a good throwing arm, and on the mound he's a great fielder. When he's pitching, it's like having an extra infielder out there.

But his fielding talent wasn't much use that inning against Harts. He threw four straight balls to their first batter.

"Hey, bring in the girl."

"Hey, girl, he's going down. He's going to slide into you."

Susie Warren shouted encouragement to Pete. Pete kicked at the dirt. He was annoyed with himself. If he had anything as a pitcher, it was control.

He went to his stretch position. He kept the runner close at first, but he still couldn't find the plate at home. His next four pitches were off target. That meant eight balls in a row. Mr. Harmon frowned. The Harts' bench shifted into high gear now.

"Pitcher's going up, up, up . . ."

"Hey, Gonzalez, don't let the girl shake you."

On the bench next to me, Tucker Harmon stirred uneasily. I kept my eyes on Pete. I couldn't believe their bench was getting to him. Pete's too cool for that, but sometimes you go out there and nothing goes right. The catcher's mitt seems tiny and the plate even smaller and your arm doesn't feel connected to your body.

Pete managed to get a strike on the third batter, but he had to lob the ball in to do it. He tried throwing hard again, and he threw two more balls. Now everyone knew the lob was coming. The batter

**140**

waited for it and then banged it up the middle to drive in a run. Only Joe Tuttle charging in hard kept the runner at first from going on to third. So they still had men on first and second and there was still nobody out.

Tucker Harmon looked at me questioningly, but I ignored him. Sid and Pete had a conference out at the mound. I guessed Sid was telling him not to lob but to chuck hard, to try and find a rhythm. But as he left the mound, Sid looked over to Mr. Harmon, and there was a catcher's look for help if I've ever seen one. Mr. Harmon didn't budge though. He was stubborn. I didn't much blame him.

Pete threw hard to the next batter and before you knew it the count was 3 and 0. Rather than walk the guy and load the bases, Pete threw a cripple, and the batter promptly hit it into left center for a double. Two more runs came in, and now the score was 7–6. We had a one-run lead. They had a man on second and still nobody out. Mr. Harmon finally called time and went out to the mound.

On the bench, Tucker turned to me. "You better warm up, Danny."

"Your dad hasn't said a word to me."

"He will."

"C'mon, Danny," Lou Salmon said. "I'll warm you up."

"Better not," I said. "It'll look like we're making decisions."

"Pete just doesn't have it today. You'll have to go in. I can't."

In our league a guy can go out of the game and

come back, but he's got to stay out for six outs. Pete hadn't got anybody out so far.

"Go ahead and warm up," Tucker said.

But something told me not to. And sure enough, Mr. Harmon left Pete in and came slowly back to the bench, studying his lineup card.

"Dad," Tucker said, "Danny Gargan's here."

"I know Danny's here, Tucker," Mr. Harmon said evenly. "I also know he quit the team."

"Can't he change his mind?"

"His isn't the only mind that has got to change," Mr. Harmon replied.

"Oh nuts," Tucker said softly. "We're going to lose."

Pete tried to bear down on the next batter. He tried too hard. He was aiming the ball now, and he couldn't find the plate. The guy walked. There were men on first and second and no outs.

"Dad," Tucker said.

"Be quiet, Tuck," Mr. Harmon said. "Just throw the ball, Pete. Just fire it in," he called out.

Pete looked over at our bench, at Mr. Harmon and then at me. He wasn't happy out there. He was sweating. Nothing was going right. I looked at Mom. She looked worried and so did Herb Warren. Out at second base, Susie Warren was shouting encouragement to Pete. The base runner was taking a big lead.

Pete's next pitch was two feet over the batter's head. Sid leaped up and hauled it down and cocked his arm to fire to third. But the Harts' guy wasn't going. And who could blame him? All their runners had to do was play it cautiously and let us hand them the ball game.

Mr. Harmon frowned. He turned to me. "Have you changed your mind about quitting, Danny?"

"Yes, sir."

"What made you change your mind?"

I hadn't expected that. How to handle it?

Pete's next pitch was in the dirt. Sid blocked it, keeping it in front of him. Our infield was silent except for Susie Warren, who kept talking about "picking cherries" or "picking peaches."

"You're no longer ashamed of having a girl on the team, is that it, Danny?"

"It wasn't the girl," I said.

He looked surprised. "What was it?"

"My mom and Susie's father. I didn't want my mom coming to our games with him."

"Oh."

He looked across the diamond at the stands. So did Tucker, Lou, and the other guys on the bench.

"But she came today anyway, didn't she?"

"Yes, sir."

It hurt to say that, but it had to be said. Suddenly, Mr. Harmon's grim face broke into a grin. "You should have told me this a long time ago."

Pete's next pitch was wide.

"I couldn't."

"Time out, ump," Mr. Harmon called. "Danny, warm up with Lou. Quickly. I'll stall out at the mound."

When the guys saw me get up with a ball in my hand, they let out a couple of whoops and hollers.

Mr. Harmon walked slowly, very slowly, out to the mound. He wasn't fooling anyone. The second trip out to the mound in an inning meant you had to take the pitcher out. But he could walk out there very slowly and talk very slowly and look over his team as though he'd put an infielder in to pitch and then call me. By that time I'd have thrown a dozen pitches, which was all I needed.

I warmed up at a short distance with Lou and after four pitches I moved back and fired a little harder. Lou was catching with his fielder's glove and wincing.

"It's OK," I said. "It's in a good cause."

"Tell that to my hand."

"All right, Gargan," the plate ump called to me, "let's get in the game."

I pretended I hadn't heard him. I wasn't ready yet. My control would be off if I went in now. I could pull a muscle. I wasn't loose yet.

And then the Harts' coach did me a favor. He came out on the field to complain.

"I heard Gargan had quit your team, Dale," he said to Mr. Harmon.

"Where did you hear that?" Mr. Harmon asked, astonished.

"All my boys were talking about it."

"Not so," Mr. Harmon said. "There was a misunderstanding, but I never put any paperwork through on Danny quitting."

"It's mighty funny, your not pitching him till now."

"He came late to the game."

Meanwhile I threw and threw and my arm started feeling in the old groove, like the hand belonged at the end of it and the ball in the hand and the fingers around the ball, and my hips were loose and I was flowing with each pitch.

"C'mon, Gargan, let's get in there," the ump said.

"All set," I told Lou Salmon, and then I ran onto the field. Pete was waiting for me at the mound with Mr. Harmon, Ed, and George. Susie Warren hung back at second. We had ten men on the field, not including Mr. Harmon. I wondered if Mr. Harmon would move Susie back to the bench and put Leo back on second.

He didn't. He fooled us all.

"Pete, why don't you sit down for a while? Leo, stay at shortstop. Susie, can you handle second?"

"Sure," she called from second.

Pete's face was red. All the kidding we'd been giving Leo, and now he was sitting down. But that's baseball. And Pete's a ball player. He went over and swatted Susie on the seat. "Look out for a double steal," he said.

"I'd like to see 'em try," Sid growled. "On me and Danny? Man, you just fire the fast one down the middle on this guy."

"Everyone, heads-up ball," Mr. Harmon said. "There's nobody out and two men on. We've got a one-run lead and the count's 3 and 0. The play's at third on a grounder. Chuck to the glove, Dan."

We all put our hands together and yelled, "Let's go," together, and then everyone went back to their positions and Pete and Mr. Harmon to the bench. I

145

was finally where I belonged: on the pitcher's mound. Mom and I looked at each other. Herb Warren was watching me too. The last time the two of them had sat together I'd lost my concentration, but it was going to be different now.

Sid hunkered down. "He'll be taking, Danny," he called out to me.

I checked the runner on second. He wasn't taking much of a lead. I looked back at Sid. The batter would be taking all the way. The odds that a pitcher, with the count 3 and 0, could come off the bench and throw a strike were not good. Their team was shouting all kinds of things at me. I didn't hear a word they said.

I looked the guy back to second a little and then I threw a grooved pitch to Sid. A smart batter would have laid wood on it, but a cautious one wouldn't. He didn't.

"Strike," the ump said.

Sid, grinning, fired the ball back to me. He signaled for another fastball. I still didn't think the Harts kid would swing. I fed him another fat one, and he let this one in for a strike too. Now I was in the driver's seat. Our guys were yelling and the Harts' bench was quiet. Their coach was angry at the batter. He was yelling, "Swing, Bobby. Swing!"

Which suited me fine. I checked the runner at second. He was taking a little longer lead now, but nothing very risky. I fired hard to Sid, not a fat pitch, but a rising fastball. It was rising out of the strike zone, but I guess that kid could still hear his coach yelling "Swing, Bobby!" because Bobby swung—about a foot under the ball.

"Way to go, Danny."

"Way to shoot that ball, Dan."

One out and their first baseman was up. He was a big left-handed batter, and the danger from him was that he could slap a ball to the opposite field. He also had power to right field. But he could be jammed.

And now was the time to jam him. I fired a fastball too tight. He ducked back. The second fastball caught the inside corner. The third fastball he swatted at and lifted a short fly ball into right field. On the bench Tucker Harmon groaned out loud. He hadn't had an opportunity out there all game, I guess. Now he was on the bench while Simple was setting himself under the ball. Simple caught it and a big cheer went up. He threw the ball back in to second. Susie caught it, checked the runner on the base, and flipped it to me.

"Way to chuck, Danny," she said.

I grinned. "Two outs," I said to her.

"Two outs," she yelled to the outfield.

"Two outs," Sid said, holding up two fingers.

Now we had them. The momentum had shifted. They'd have to take chances now. They'd have to put pressure on me. Their bench was shrieking, trying to rattle me. If they didn't score this inning, they never would.

The batter was their third baseman, a good hitter, a pull hitter. I looked over at Ed and he nodded and moved toward the line. Leo, who wasn't used to playing shortstop, asked me where he should play. "In the hole." I looked at Susie Warren. She had instinctively moved closer to second base to keep the runner close. I didn't think he'd be going. Not with two outs. But you never know when the other team gets desperate.

I looked down at Sid. He was signaling the fastball and making motions for it to be outside. He was expecting a double steal. I went to my stretch position. To my amazement, the runner on second was taking an enormous lead. Maybe he thought he'd take advantage of Leo playing in the hole and a girl covering second base.

I stepped off the mound. He ran back to second.

"Time," I called, and motioned for Susie to come over. She came and so did Leo and George.

"If this guy takes another lead like that, let's pick him off."

She nodded, but I could tell from her eyes she didn't know how to work it. We hadn't practiced pickoff plays with her.

"Here's how it'll go. I'll take my signal from Sid. Then I'll look back at that guy. If I think we ought to try to pick him off, I'll touch the back of my cap. Then I'll go to my stretch. When my hands come down to my chest like this . . . you got it?"

"Yeah."

"We'll both count, one potato, two potato, three potato, four. On four, I'm going to turn and throw to second. You cut for that base on four. You'll be there with the ball."

She looked like she didn't believe me. "In Ohio
. . ." she started to say.

"You're in Michigan now," I snapped. "Let's do it
together. OK, my hands come down and . . ."

We chanted together softly, "One potato, two potato, three potato, four . . ."

"On four?"

"I cut."

"And don't forget to tag him out," Leo said, grinning.

"Danny's dad taught us that one," George said.
He was grinning too. "Next time you can tell us
how you did it in Ohio."

She blushed.

"Let's go," the ump shouted. "Batter up."

We went back to our positions.

"Two away," Sid yelled. "No batter. Play at any
base. No sweat. Way ahead. Shoot it to me, Danny
man. Fire to my glove."

I took my sign from Sid and then, before going to
my stretch, I looked back at the runner. He was
moving off, farther and farther. His eye was on Leo,
not on Susie Warren. You steal on a girl.

I touched the back of my cap and then slowly
went to my stretch and slowly, very slowly, brought
my hands down to my chest. One potato, two potato,
three potato, four—

I whirled and fired at the bag. There was a flurry
of bodies out there. The runner desperately trying
to get back, diving in head first, Susie diving to
catch the ball. She'd been slow getting there. The
ball bounced off her glove and into center field.

149

Their bench yelled, "Run," but the runner couldn't run. He couldn't move at all. Susie was lying on top of him.

The Harts' coach was screaming interference. Susie got up slowly. Joe Tuttle threw the ball in to Leo, who was grinning as he caught it.

"Hey, you really fall for girls, don't you, Fodale?" he asked the runner, who'd crawled back to the bag.

"That was interference, ump," the Harts' coach shouted.

Susie snapped her bubble gum. "Sorry," she said to me.

I caught the ball from Leo. "We'll try it again," I said with a laugh.

Our bench was laughing. Even Mr. Harmon was smiling. In the stands Mr. Warren was shaking his head. I guess he'd always known Susie was a tough competitor, but maybe he didn't know how tough she was till today.

"Play ball. Batter up," the ump said. He hadn't the nerve to call interference. It would be a tough call even for a professional ump to make. It's a judgment of intentions more than anything else.

I looked back at Susie. She looked at me. The runner was dusting himself off on the bag. He was taking angry swipes at his pants. He was sore. A girl keeping him from going to third, maybe even scoring. He'd really stick it to us now!

I winked at Susie. She winked back.

I looked in at Sid and then casually looked back. He was taking a long lead. I touched my cap again. Check it, Susie. Check it!

Then I went to my stretch, pulled my hands down to my chest, and started counting again. On the fourth potato I whirled and fired, and this time Susie was there. It wasn't even close. He was out by two feet.

"Way to go," Joe Tuttle yelled, and banged Susie on the back.

George slapped her too. Leo punched her in the arm. "Way to play, man," he said.

She ran in quickly, chewing her gum hard, looking to neither left nor right.

"Good play, second base," Mr. Harmon said. And to me, "Nice work out there, Danny. I'm glad you're back."

"So am I."

We beat Harts 11-6, getting four more runs out of just sheer happiness.

# 15.

MY STORY REALLY ENDS here 'cause what followed doesn't have an end yet, at least not one I can see.

After the ball game, Mr. Harmon, all emotional, shook everyone's hand. We shook hands with the Harts and kidded them. They shook hands with Susie, even though they didn't want to. Their coach griped to Mr. Harmon about "the stunt that girl pulled on us."

"What girl?" Mr. Harmon asked. "Oh, you mean our second baseman?"

Then Mr. Harmon sat us down and told us he was proud of us and that we were a ball club again, a tight team, a strong team. Everyone had played well. Susie Warren was going to be a backup infielder, and if anyone got hurt, she'd start. "If you want my advice," Mr. Harmon added solemnly, "none of you infielders will get hurt."

Everyone laughed, even the infielders, though I'm not sure they thought it was that funny.

"Danny's back," Mr. Harmon said, "not that he ever left. Though he gave us a scare. I'm calling a practice for Saturday morning. We got a big game Monday against Wilson Furniture. Who can't make the practice?"

Everyone could. Winners always practice.

"Now, the Dairy Queens are on me."

"And on me too," said a voice from behind the bench. It was Herb Warren. Mom was with him, looking at me. I wondered how long they'd been there.

"I'd like to buy some too, Mr. Harmon," Mrs. Grayson said. "I think everyone's forgotten that Sid hit a home run today."

"Did you hit a home run today, Sid?" Warren McDonald asked.

"I don't remember any home runs today," Leo said.

"All I remember is a girl flattening out a Harts runner," Ed Farkas said. "We ought to have that girl starting."

"Aw, cut it out, Ed," Leo said.

"Do we have enough cars?" Mr. Warren asked. "I can take five."

"Let's go, guys," Pete said, and he ran for the parking lot. A bunch of guys ran after him. I walked over to Mom and Herb Warren. He stuck out his hand.

"That was one of the best relief jobs I've ever seen, Dan."

I shook his hand.

"Thanks."

We started walking toward the parking lot. Susie was ahead of us, walking with Tucker Harmon and Warren McDonald. Tuck was carrying the bag.

"I was surprised to see you, Dan," Mom said quietly.

I felt my face turn red.

"Your mother told me you'd quit," Herb Warren said.

And redder.

"She didn't tell me why."

I looked up at Mom and then at him. They were waiting for me. If I didn't tell him anything, I knew it would be all right too. But now I wanted to tell him.

"I quit because I didn't want you and Mom coming to games together. When Susie made the team, I knew you would."

"I see . . ." He looked from me to Mom. It seemed to me he looked at Mom a long while. "But you came anyway, Nancy."

And now it was Mom's turn to blush. "I like baseball," she said.

Herb Warren laughed, and so did I. And suddenly everything was in place again.

"Well," Herb Warren said quietly. "Any way you look at it, it was quite a game. How did you think Susie played, Dan?"

"Real good."

"I think she did all right for her first time out. She was plenty scared, I can tell you."

"She didn't look it."

"She's a good actress. A lot of playing ball well is acting a part."

Dad used to say that too, I thought.

"Hey, Mr. Warren, how do you get this tailgate down?" Tucker Harmon called out. He'd got rid of the equipment bag and wanted to ride with Susie. It was funny.

"You need a key," Herb Warren said. "I've got it."

He went ahead of us. Mom turned to me. "What made you change your mind, Dan?"

I hesitated. "Heck, you were coming to the game with him anyway."

She looked at me. She could read me. She knew how stubborn I was. I wouldn't have come on just that.

"Well, there was something else . . . ." I took a deep breath. "I called Dad in Chicago."

She didn't say anything. She just watched me.

"It cost a fortune."

"I said you could always call him. Did he tell you to play?"

"No. He would have, I know, but I didn't tell him I quit. We didn't talk about me at all. He . . . uh . . . Mom, Dad's getting married again."

Mom missed her stride a little. It wasn't much, but it was there. When she spoke though, her voice was calm. "I'm glad for him."

"I told him you were doing all right too, Mom. I

told him all about Herb Warren. I told him what a terrific guy Mr. Warren is, and what a good ball player he was, and how he writes stories and things. I told him you were real happy now and—"

Mom stopped me by taking my hand. "Danny . . ."

"It's true, isn't it?"

"Yes," she said. She cleared her throat. "It's just hearing you say it. Excuse me."

She took out a handkerchief and blew her nose.

"Are you OK?"

"I must have got some dust in my nose. I'm OK. Are you?"

"Yeah."

I was, too. Walking with Mom to Mr. Warren's station wagon, watching Susie and the guys horse around, knowing we'd won a big one, coming back, doing it the hard way. I was more than OK. I was happy.

We went for Dairy Queens and afterward Mr. Warren dropped off a load of guys and then he and Susie drove us home.

"Would you like to come in?" Mom asked, and I thought she was being very polite.

"Not now," Mr. Warren said, smiling, "but may I give you a call later?"

"Of course," Mom said.

"Good game, Dan," he said.

"Thanks. Good game, Susie," I said to her.

"Yeah," she said, and blew her last bubble of the day at me. "Good game," she said, and snapped it off.

Mr. Warren laughed, and they drove off. Mom and I watched them go.

"She sure gets a lot out of one stick of gum," I said.

"Doesn't she?" Mom laughed. We went inside and sat down.

"Dan," Mom said.

"Yeah?" I knew what was coming.

"Did your father sound happy?"

I nodded.

"I'm happy for him then. I really am."

"She's got kids too. Little kids."

"That's good. He ought to have children around admiring him."

"I admire him, Mom. I'm his son. I'm always going to be his son, aren't I? No matter what happens. If you marry Herb Warren, I'm always going to be Matt Gargan's boy, aren't I?"

"Of course you are. You always will be."

"I hope you and Mr. Warren get married too."

Mom smiled. "You do go from one extreme to the other, Danny Gargan. Well, all I can say is, we'll see. I'm happy right now and I refuse to think too far ahead. Now, would you like some supper?"

"Sure, but I wanna watch the White Sox game on TV."

"All right, I'll call you when it's ready."

"Can I have some pop now?"

"Just one. I don't want you to ruin your appetite."

Everything had changed and nothing had changed. I went to the refrigerator and got myself a cold can of pop. Then I found the White Sox game on TV and stretched my legs and drank my pop. It felt good dripping into my thirsty body.

I watched the Sox-Brewers game and waited for a shot of Dad in the bull pen. But the Sox pitcher was doing OK and there were no bull pen shots. While I waited I relived our own game. In the inning I came in, I got the first guy on a strikeout and had a one-and-one count on the second guy and was getting ready to throw an inside fastball for him to pop up to Simple, when someone hit a ground foul to the White Sox bull pen and there was Dad, hunkered down with that big old familiar back and throwing the ball slowly with that old familiar throw. My heart skipped a beat watching him those couple of seconds, and then the camera flashed back to the diamond.

And Mom called me in for supper.

# About the Author

ALFRED SLOTE lives in Ann Arbor, Michigan, and is the author of a number of sports books for young people: TONY AND ME; HANG TOUGH, PAUL MATHER; MY FATHER, THE COACH; THE BIGGEST VICTORY; JAKE; STRANGER ON THE BALL CLUB. A former baseball coach and player and the father of three children, he draws his material from first-hand knowledge.